HELIGOLAND

Shena Mackay is the author of two novellas, eight previous novels and four collections of short stories. Her novel *The Orchard on Fire* was shortlisted for the Booker Prize in 1996.

By the same author

Dust Falls on Eugene Schlumberger/Toddler on the Run
Music Upstairs
Old Crow
An Advent Calendar
Babies in Rhinestones
A Bowl of Cherries
Redhill Rococo
Dreams of Dead Women's Handbags
Dunedin
The Laughing Academy
Collected Stories
Such Devoted Sisters (*editor*)
The Orchard on Fire
Friendship (*editor*)
The Artist's Widow
The Worlds Smallest Unicorn

HELIGOLAND

SHENA MACKAY

Jonathan Cape
London

Published by Jonathan Cape 2003

2 4 6 8 10 9 7 5 3 1

First published in Great Britain in 2003 by
Jonathan Cape
Random House, 20 Vauxhall Bridge Road, London SW1V 2SA

Random House Australia (Pty) Limited
20 Alfred Street, Milsons Point, Sydney,
New South Wales 2061, Australia

Random House New Zealand Limited
18 Poland Road, Glenfield,
Auckland 10, New Zealand

Random House South Africa (Pty) Limited
Endulini, 5A Jubilee Road, Parktown 2193, South Africa

The Random House Group Limited Reg. No. 954009
www.randomhouse.co.uk

A CIP catalogue record for this book is available from the British Library

ISBN 0-224-07251-X

Papers used by Random House are natural, recyclable products made from wood grown in sustainable forests; the manufacturing processes conform to the environmental regulations of the country of origin

Typeset by Palimpsest Book Production Limited,
Polmont, Stirlingshire
Printed and bound in Great Britain by
Mackays of Chatham Plc, Chatham, Kent

For
Edwin Peter Smith & Eleanor Shena Clark

I

'Soon be home now. Soon be nice and warm. Soon be home, soon be nice and warm.' The aunt kept up her mantra through the blizzard while the black pram bucked and slithered and ploughed into snowdrifts.

'Niceawaarm,' wailed the child as the aunt pushed. She dragged the pram's impacted wheels blindly like a white horse, her head bowed in the maelstrom of blown and falling snow. The child was two years old but the pram was the only means by which the aunt could transport her, with the rations, the heavy new battery for the wireless, firewood and paraffin. Flakes swirled in under the hood and piled up on the apron in a white blanket, and the wind droned and howled, whipping away the aunt's tears from the effort and the pain of the intense cold, sculpting new banks and cornices to overhang and block what used to be the road, bulking into white shapes that might be hidden bushes or hedges, or sheer cliffs of snow. At each step her snow-filled boots sank; at times they were pulled right off and she had to dig them out with her hands. More than once she measured her length and almost overturned the pram. Frozen stiff, rabbits lay by the wayside and starving deer had stripped the bark from the tree trunks above the snowline, leaving them palely exposed and dying. The long black twigs of the weeping birch were gripped in the ice of the loch.

'Nice-a-waaarm . . .' The child's response was shaken out of her in a shuddering lamb's bleat as home at last they came to the cottage friezed with icicles, bumping past the drainpipe whose starburst of ice promised eventual fracture and flood, under the glassy daggers bristling in the porch, to the front door where a mass of snow waited to force its way in with them.

Inside, the aunt unpinned the scarf criss-crossed round the child's coat, removed the coat and bonnet, peeled off sodden mittens and sucked the tips of purple fingers for a moment to thaw them, before kneeling to unbutton the white corduroy leggings. Her own chilblained fingers were bent into claws from gripping the pram handle, prickling and throbbing as they unfroze, fumbling down the rows of tiny buttons, without pinching the child's legs once. The child clasped her arms round the aunt's neck to steady herself, resting blue-black hair against wet red-gold, and the aunt licked a melted snowflake from her eyelashes with the tip of her tongue and planted a kiss on each icy knee.

The kitchen filled with the smoke that, blown back by the wind, gusted over the edge of the newspaper the aunt was holding across the range to blaze up the fire; a lump of snow fell down the chimney but the fire caught. Snow melted in the kettle, the flames burned steadily in their glass shades while beyond the orange hemisphere of the radio's dial and the snowlight of the window the moon climbed through freezing curds.

The Great Winter of 1946–7 preserved Rowena Snow's first memories in ice but ever afterwards, at odd moments, a flash of gold, silver or deep-dyed colour would tantalise her memory, hinting at an earlier consciousness. Rowena associated snow, and also rhododendrons, the leaves weighted with frozen crystals, the crimson and scarlet flowers, with her childhood in Scotland; she had no recollection of the foothills of the Himalayas where she was born or of the ship that brought her as an orphaned baby from India. Still, out of the blue, a cut-glass dish of ice cream streaked with raspberry syrup, a circle of fallen blossoms round the base of an azalea or a bangle on a wrist might make an elliptical reference to something forgotten, but Rowena could no more seize their allusions than a baby can grasp the rings tied with a ribbon to the bars of its cot, just out of reach.

Half a century or so on from that first remembered winter, Rowena Snow was walking home one summer night after spending the day with her friend Sylvia Dunlop. Rowena had been orphaned for the second time at the age of eight, by the sudden death of her aunt, and transplanted, again with no say in the matter, to a chestnut grove in southern England, in which part of the world she had remained.

As she walked past honeysuckle snaking through the slats of fences bulging with Russian vines and tiny grapes, flowering rockery plants cascading over garden walls, Rowena crushed blue-green bittersweet oil of rue in her fingertips. She was responsible for the existence of Iris, the youngest Dunlop girl. If George Dunlop had not fallen in love with her seventeen years ago, Iris would not have been born. She imagined a grey space devoid of Iris. One chair fewer at the table. A voice unheard.

Rowena had long since acknowledged that rather than starring as the romantic female lead in her own drama, she had been merely a catalyst in the Dunlop saga. Although Sylvia never knew the reason for George's sudden distraction and neglect, she had fallen into a deep depression. Their two girls were both at school and Sylvia's doctor suggested that another baby might be the answer to her problem. So now George and Sylvia had this tall Iris with a butterfly tattoo on one golden shoulder and hair that caught the sun like dragonflies' wings, who couldn't decide whether to make art or music her career, and Rowena had a carrier bag of the Dunlops' runner beans and vine tomatoes.

Nevertheless, momentarily alone in their garden, she had become conscious, in the play of light on water and leaves, of a pointillistic universe and its perpetual growth and motion. Nothing was static, from the water boatmen and weeds on the pond, the shining skin of the frogs' heads breaking the surface, to the polychromatic glitter of the starling's feathers, on the chimney where a bramble waved against the sky. Transfixed, she noted the living material of the clouds, spiders' webs, each filament of the cat's fur and dandelions' parachutes; she could almost see the lichen creeping on the brickwork, mortar crumbling, yellow invading the white paint of the garden furniture, sap, chlorophyll, cellulose at work, almost hear the tripartite lacquered pods of irises creaking open, the cuckoo pint shuffling back its green cowls to show green berries, ferns uncurling, the poppies shrugging off their hoods. She felt the force and determination to live and propagate in every blade and spore, in the unimaginable insect brains that drove their threadlike legs. Now she was carrying joy home with her bag of garden produce, through the cedar and eucalyptus-blue evening.

Round the corner thudded a red Mercedes slamming out rap, crammed with boys; it overtook her, reversed and pulled up. Instinctively, Rowena shifted her bag to the other shoulder, twisted the handles of the carrier round her hand so that it could serve as a weapon, assessed the height of the wall alongside her, the distance to the gate, and dealt with the decision to run or stand her ground. One of two youths in the passenger seat stuck out his head.

'White Horse Lane?' he yelled over the aggressive vocal, drum and bass.

Smiling with relief that they weren't going to attack her, Rowena pointed them in the right direction. As she walked on, saddened that youth is the enemy unless proved otherwise, something hard struck the back of her head. She clapped her hand to her skull. Shattered bone fragmented under her fingers. Slowly she withdrew her hand, and stared, at bright yellow blood and jellied brain fluid in her palm. Then broken egg slid down her neck, down the back of her dress, down her leg, as the car screeched into a U-turn of whooping laughter and noise.

Fury and hate surged through her; she imagined the red car smashed up against a lamp-post. Standing there, in the indifference of the windows and closed doors and calm gardens, a blackbird singing on a satellite dish the only witness to the assault, she scrubbed away the slime with a tissue.

Was it personal? Racial? You had to think in terms

of black and white, although she was neither. The ugly words Paki-bashing flashed into her mind. Was it random? Had the boys piled into a car armed with an egg, looking for any likely victim? She imagined a conversation in a pub: 'What shall we do now, lads? Who fancies going egging? It'll be a laugh!'

Well, people could be stabbed or kicked to death for a laugh, so perhaps she had been lucky to escape with only egg on her face, so to speak. But the impact of the missile still throbbed on the back of her head. She had felt fragments of her own skull and her blood glooping through her fingers.

If it *had* been a bullet, that's how she would have died, sprawled among the Dunlops' bloody runner beans and squashed tomatoes. People did die like that; a faint yelp of surprise, and the pavement crashing up to meet them, all their business unfinished. I was just in the wrong place at the wrong time, she told herself, but that thought opened on to the bleak landscape where she was always alone, and she saw a weeping birch tree with its twigs frozen into the ice of a loch, like a girl who bowed her head over the water to wash her long dark hair, and found it gripped fast by an enchanter's spell. She saw her aunt sprawled in the green bracken, poleaxed by an aneurysm. Hoisting her bag on to her shoulder again, she plodded on. A voice in her head sneered, '"And there goes Miss Bell with her fusty old Nut".' Blake's sinister little ballad had struck fear into her heart the first time she read it, as if it was a warning of derision to come, just as Walter de la Mare's mocking fairy had called her to the window which opened on to her future.

Then she was safe, crunching over the shingle of the land-locked bay. Glimmering through the trees, the Nautilus waited, luminous in the gloaming, a vast pearly shell throwing lustre over tamarisks, brushwood and high leaves. Rowena followed the links of the chain which, half submerged in pebbles, looped the breakwater, and led to an anchor resting at an angle on its curve a few yards from the entrance of the building. She stood still, with her hand on the anchor, taking deep breaths of resinous air, letting her rage and humiliation drain into the iron. Then she sat on the breakwater for a long time, watching the moon. At last, feeling like a hermit crab scuttling back to its refuge, she fitted her key to the lock.

The final watery phrase of 'Sailing By' floated from Francis Campion's radio, leaving a trail of bubbles in the greenish light while Rowena climbed the spiral stair. As she passed the old poet's door, she heard the muffled benign syllables of the shipping forecast.

No more Heligoland, though. Heligoland was never mentioned now. Political and meteorological maps had been redrawn. Heligoland, or Helgoland, did exist, she knew from checking in an atlas, a small island in the North Sea belonging to Germany, off the mouth of the River Elbe, but the Heligoland of her heart was, as the imagination makes possible, both an island over unnavigable seas and a fairground roundabout. Her childhood world had been destroyed as if by a hurricane roaring out of blue skies, and so she could never hear the shipping forecast without becoming for a moment a child in a kitchen with her beloved aunt.

The six o'clock news, gale warnings, reports of escaped convicts, police messages for people whose relatives were dangerously ill, the sports results with the strange and magical names of football teams and racehorses, all streamed in a procession of living pictures through her mind as she held the toasting fork to the flames, and thus her Heligoland was conceived by the association of sound and colour. In her mind's eye H was grey, ergo she saw a merry-go-round of galloping horses all as grey as the North Sea, laughing horses with sculpted manes and tails prancing on their silver poles, whirling in a spume of misty waves, and also an island in the fog beyond the Hebrides and Finisterre. Heligoland remains for Rowena a hazy, faraway, indefinable place of solace and reunion.

When she closed her chamber door her heart leaped up at the sight of her new rainbow duster with an extending handle, and she showered and went to bed in anticipation of winding hitherto unreachable cobwebs round its dust-magnetic spiracles.

Strictly speaking, Gus Crabb, a dealer rather than practitioner in arts and crafts, did not qualify for residency at the Nautilus, but Celeste liked him, and thought his name was amusingly appropriate for the marine scheme of things there. He rolled a joint, waiting for a *Seinfeld* repeat with the sound turned down, half listening to a Miles Davis CD, aware of Rowena's bathwater cascading into the drain, reaching for the remote to zap the contingent of pensioners from the West Midlands who, dressed only in thongs, were weaving a juddering conga through a Marbella nightclub. Now Rowena would be lying neatly in her bed in those lavender-sprigged pyjamas he'd noticed hanging on the line. The shirts she had ironed for him had reappeared on a hanger at his door, full of fresh air. He imagined her sleeping like a child, or a nun in a cell, with her glossy hair brushed and small brown hands folded, dark lashes resting above the curve of her cheekbone. What was her provenance? What was her date?

There was something familiar about Rowena, a green prickly burr that his mind couldn't grasp, a look, a gesture that almost opened a door on the past, then closed it abruptly. He was aware of it when he first saw her in the Gipsy Rose Café back in January. He'd been showing Rita, the proprietress, a Victorian ostrich egg he'd just picked up, when he'd noticed a woman sitting alone, watching them. She'd been there again a few weeks later, reading the classifieds in the local paper. They'd got chatting; she was fed up with her flat and her job, and on impulse he'd told her about the Nautilus. Thinking about Rowena diverted his thoughts from somebody else, Lois, who had this cute way of taking off her T-shirt, pulling it over her head like a little boy, that still made him smile, even though she'd ruined his life.

Gus's apartment was gradually becoming a stock-room for Crabb's Antiques, his shop near Gipsy Hill, with cardboard boxes ever narrowing the living space. His bed was heaped with the day's bric-a-brac; eventually he would lift the bedspread off like a hammock and dump the whole clanking lot on the floor, chrome bathroom fittings pitted by the moisture of generations' ablutions, snakeskin shoes with heels like fangs, soup tureen, cheese dish, bundles of cutlery secured with rubber bands, a copy of *The Hanging Gardens of Penge* by Francis Campion, inscribed by the author 'To Maud with affection'.

* * *

Francis Campion had climbed obediently between the sheets for *The Late Book* and at last he snuggled down to the radio's lullaby, 'Sailing By', unwinding his legs, which had twisted into a corkscrew. If he opened his fingers a little bit more he could see Louis MacNeice's hat on the door. Francis couldn't sleep until the BBC had tucked up its listeners with the shipping forecast and the National Anthem. Even so, he was often woken at two by 'Lillibullero', to find himself in the throes of the World Service.

He took a rather sardonic view of his dependence on dear old Ronald Binge's 'Sailing By': so quintessentially middlebrow and Middle England, but then, his happiest years were spent in Broadcasting House, commissioning and producing drama, talks and poetry programmes – hence the hat of his old colleague Louis MacNeice – fire-watching and Caversham Park in the war, monitoring enemy broadcasts, a stint or two as a sub-editor on the *Listener*. The 1950s had found him coating nuts and fondants with chocolate at the Payne's sweet factory on Croydon Road, employment which had inspired his most anthologised poem, 'Poppets', a celebration of the eponymous confectionery and the interlocking plastic beads worn by his female fellow-workers. He could still hear the girls' and women's voices singing along to 'Workers' Playtime' on the wireless. How sweet in retrospect were those Light Programme, chocolate-scented days when he'd cycled home to the Nautilus with assorted misshapes rattling in his saddlebag.

Nowadays he listened mostly to music, since the old Home Service had become, by and large, Radio Bore, with its websites and fact sheets, churning out consumer anxiety and doom from every corner of the globe, spreading alarm and despondency, stranding him on a spit of land ever eroded by a philistine sea, with his telescope trained on the past. Somewhere out there on the airwaves was a simple nostrum, a herb of grace that would have been balm to his hurt soul, but where was the listener to *Poetry Please* who would request a poem by Francis Campion?

Increasingly, this survivor in a once polyglot shelltopia was aware of a creeping xenophobia that was turning him into a parochial old tortoise. He was glad Celeste couldn't read his mind. Celeste saw good in everybody and believed the most abysmal reprobates to be on the side of the angels. The covers of Francis's books, faded to the colour of dusty tea and embossed with the Nautilus Press colophon, enclosed experimental verse and political satire as well as lyrical and pastoral poems, but now that the world had gone beyond satire, he saw how his youthful absurdism was just a product of its era, a minute, odd-shaped piece in a jigsaw puzzle. And that his imagism, and all his isms, were regarded now, if at all, as merely period pieces. Each stage of his development had led not to some glorious late flowering, and public recognition, of his gift, but only to a stint on the committee of the society which was widely referred to by its unofficial acronym, DAMS, taken from Wordsworth's observation that 'We poets in our youth begin in gladness: / But thereof comes in the end despondency and madness.'

Next to his own stood the Collected Works, in Gaelic and English, of his old friend Magnus Scrabster, that scrawny island sheep whose long face Francis dearly would have loved to see again. After the war, Magnus had chosen the better part, rejecting the metropolis, his roots gripping ever tighter the granite beneath his native soil, piercing the stone and entwining the skeletons of animals and birds, the skulls of his forefathers. Francis envied Magnus his sea, skies and rocks, the skirl of skuas, the coronachs and pibrochs, the standing stones, the Gaelic that linked him to history, and even the wee wifie Jean, who had never cared much for Francis.

Strangers and change. Francis mourned the parade of shops which had been part of his routine for years. The little community where he felt at home had vanished. The other day he'd taken his spectacles to the optician's to have a lens which had fallen out replaced, and found himself, purblind, in a nail parlour. Familiar premises were boarded up or refurbished as inconvenience stores where, to the succession of proprietors, Francis Campion was just another doddery geezer with a string bag. Fortunately, though, the new housekeeper's young legs could take her further afield.

Recently, Francis's general malaise had presented a fresh symptom. He was taunted by his own juvenilia. Suddenly, out of the ether, sprang an aborted verse, declaiming itself in a sarcastic voice sibilant with adolescent thees and thous, making him wince and even groan aloud. A litter of alliteration. A hundred wastepaper baskets testifying against him.

Several tubs of pills stood on his bedside table but none contained a remedy for his anomie. 'Old men go mad at night,' Tennessee Williams had observed before his comparatively youthful demise from choking on the cap of a bottle of sleeping pills, alone in a hotel room. You couldn't open these childproof containers with your teeth if you tried, although you might cut your fingers on the plastic seal. *Quem Jupiter vult perdere dementat prius*. Of course, the gods had always had it in for poets, but in Francis's observation the majority of old men go mad without divine intervention. He could write a book on mad old men running amok, the mad old men of London in the crazy baseball caps of their dotage and ladies' raincoats from charity shops, the roaring drunks who fall out of the bus at the wrong stop, shouting, 'Thank you, Driver,' so that nobody will know they're drunk. Men without women, going to seed.

However, rather than frittering away such time as he had left on misanthropic verses that would only mock him after he had gone, he must concentrate on his memoirs, *Take Me Back To The Gaierty Hotel*. But how laborious writing prose was; the slippery narrative thread that kept breaking and getting knotted up. Odd, though, how old women in general seemed to retain a better grasp of things even when widowed, not losing touch with soap and water, detergent, hairdressers and all sartorial sense.

'Sailing By' brought Francis consolation in the form of his own coffin, shipshape, of polished wood and gleaming brass, gliding along runners, disappearing through closing curtains, launched into eternity with little coloured flags waving cheerily, as if for a regatta. He thought that he would be able to put to sea with equanimity if the band on the diminishing harbourfront was playing him out to 'Sailing By'.

Celeste Zylberstein, *fons et origo* of the Nautilus, had dozed off over a book, in bed, propped up by pillows.

The light from her reading lamp gave her hair a bluish tone and a succession of heavy earrings had almost indiscernibly elongated her lobes. Celeste's eyelids flickered behind her spectacles and in her half-sleep she was aware of her building's nocturnal sounds, and the silence pounding like surf in the empty rooms.

Two more vacancies since the defection of Frau Stumpfenhose and Fräulein Bustenhalter, as Gus Crabb insisted on calling them, to sheltered accommodation in Bromley, where by all accounts they were living the life of Old Mother Riley. So much for their lame excuse that increasing infirmity made the Nautilus untenable: she'd caught them on daytime television, making an exhibition of themselves on a show hosted from the Glades Shopping Centre by some capering nebbish. Formerly perfectly acceptable potters, they'd materialised on the screen in dirndl and lederhosen, hopping about in the hand-clapping dance from *Hansel and Gretel*, exposing not only feet but knees and well-slapped thighs of clay. For this we pay our licence fee?

Celeste stirred at the reassuring crunch of Rowena's footsteps, the silence that suggested she had paused by the anchor, recognising it as symbolic of a safe berth, and so, please God, would stay. She crossed her fingers on which the rings hung loosely.

Celeste's back was curved but, like the Nautilus, she had a core of steel. This building inspired by a spiral shell with a series of air-filled chambers was the fulfilment of a dream. In collaboration with her late husband Arkady, she had designed it on modernist and Utopian principles, presided over its opening in 1937, and lived within at the centre of a floating community of cosmopolitan refugees, dispossessed artists and intellectuals for whom the anchor at its entrance became emblematic in wartime and exile. In some lights the anodised carapace had a viridescent sheen; at other times it gleamed like pearl.

The great shell housed, in addition to its residential chambers, a laundry, a kitchen, a communal dining room where guests were welcome, studios and workshops, a printing press, and the Nautilus Bar, like a glass and steel aquarium, with its ultramarine piano. *Chambered nautilus* – a cephalopod nautilus pompilius of the Pacific and Indian Oceans, having a partitioned shell lined with a pearly layer. Also known as *pearly nautilus.* And *Nautilus*, to Celeste's distress, was the name given to the world's first nuclear submarine.

The surrounding beach had been transported piecemeal from Dungeness in lorryloads of shingle, with a section of breakwater, flotsam and jetsam, coastal plants, green glass fishing floats and the anchor on its chain. Francis Campion had dug up a pair of 'slats', the slabs of wood that Dungeness people tie under their boots with tarred twine to facilitate walking on the deeply shelving shingle; he wore them still, and called them 'The Shoes of the Fisherman'.

North London had its Isokon, south London its Nautilus, and although time had dealt more kindly with the latter, age was corroding its complex interior and, by the start of the new millennium, there were few visitors, the ultramarine piano in the Nautilus Bar was dumb and all the original residents but Celeste and Francis Campion were long gone, and ideas and ideologies were broken glass and crumpled paper.

2

Rowena slept, not peacefully as Gus imagined, but restlessly, dreaming of another establishment, another community. Chestnuts, the progressive boarding school founded during the war by Clifford and Wendy Waddilove, who had no children of their own; Wendy, whose lap made a comfortable hammock for a small child to nest in, and rangy Clifford with his scarlet waistcoat and Brylcreemed hair that fell in a curtain over his face as he supervised the Wednesday Pillow Fight or ran about the sports field, constantly interchanging pipe and referee's whistle. Chestnuts, many-chimneyed, red-brick and tile hung, condemned by the local community, stood at the end of an avenue of horse chestnuts and both conkers and sweet chestnuts studded the grounds which backed on to farmland. Its pupils were categorised by size, into Sticky Buds, Candles and Conkers. To Chestnuts it was that Rowena was dispatched when Aunt Mysie died, for who else would take her but Mysie's old university friend Wendy Waddilove? Lady Grouseclaw up at the Castle where Mysie, accompanied by Rowena, was governess to her youngest son Hamish, had organised the whole betrayal.

'The rose of all the world is not for me: / I want for my part, / Only the little white rose of

Scotland, / That smells sharp and sweet – and breaks the heart'; Rowena kept the poem among her mind's secret treasures but she had never returned to Scotland. Her one attempt to go back had ended in defeat. It took place three weeks after Clifford Waddilove met her off the Flying Scotsman and delivered her to his wife with the mortifying words, 'I've brought you our new little Sticky Bud.'

Rowena had planned to find one of the remote abandoned crofts she had seen from the train window on her journey south, and live there, on roots and berries and water from the burn, with rabbits and sheep for company. They would be her friends, soft-coated friends with kind faces. Nobody must ever see her; 'For if they find us in the glen, our blood will stain the heather,' she told Angus, her blue velvet sailor doll, whose celluloid face had been trodden in by a boy called Heinz who always wet his bed. Nobody, that is, except someone like Alan Breck, on the run from the Redcoats, whom she would shelter and defend. Heinz had deliberately tied on his football boots and then kicked Angus round the room. Angus, chosen by Rowena and Mysie from all the dolls in Jenners of Edinburgh. Who had been with her when Mysie was dead in the bracken.

That lunchtime, always a movable feast at Chestnuts, Rowena complained of a headache and went to lie down. Then, after placing two pillows and a football under the covers, she bundled up Angus, a photograph, a slab of Wendy's turnip cake, a medicine bottle filled with water and her tartan penknife, and set off down the twisting avenue leading from Chestnuts to the five-barred gate that opened on to Station Road. She needed only the clothes she stood up in, for she was going to weave a cloak from bracken, but she had tied her pink ribbon in her hair. There was 2s 11d in her purse, which would be enough for a ticket to London, and then it would be easy to get on the train for Scotland by tagging behind some family in the crowd of passengers. She would hide from the guard in the lavatory and jump off when the train slowed down.

Rowena turned the corner. There, sitting on the gate, blocking the sky, was Clifford Waddilove. His big red waistcoat extinguishing all hope.

He took his pipe from his mouth, saying, '"There was a naughty boy and a naughty boy was he, / He ran away to Scotland the people there to see . . ."'

Rowena glared at him. 'Brace the eyeball stiff as drum, that the tear may never come.' Naughty was a word never heard at Chestnuts. Heinz hadn't even got into trouble for ruining Angus's face for ever. She was not going to say sorry, because she wasn't. She realised Cliff was saying a poem. The sweetness of his tobacco mingled with the rank-sweet meadow smell.

'"And he found that the ground was as hard, / That a yard was as long / That a song was as merry,"' he twinkled on.

The poem was yards long, winding on like the road. She wanted Cliff to shut up but she wished he'd go on for ever because she was afraid of what would happen when he finished. She felt stupid standing there, scratching an insect bite on her leg. She imagined plunging her tartan penknife into Cliff's chest.

'"And he stood in his shoes and he wondered, / He stood in his shoes and he wondered,"' concluded Cliff at last and popped his pipe back in his mouth.

'How did you know I was running away to Scotland?' asked Rowena.

'Perhaps the red-and-white spotted bundle on a stick had something to do with it,' he chuckled. 'I think we should take Wendy back her scarf, don't you? It's rather a nice one.'

Rowena, not saying she'd realised it was daft and was going to chuck it away, scuffled the dust in shame at the thought of Aunt Mysie watching the scene from heaven. 'Sharing' at Chestnuts meant letting other people snatch and break your things, but it seemed you weren't allowed to share the Waddiloves' stuff. Now they would know she didn't like them. She couldn't care less. She hated them. She hated England. She scratched the insect bite until it bled. She had heard one of the big Conkers saying that property is theft, and now she had been caught thieving Wendy's property. Well, they could kill her for all she cared, but Cliff had jumped down from the gate and was handing her a dock leaf.

'It's not a nettle sting. I wonder –' said Rowena.

'What do you wonder, if the ground is as hard?'

'It is. No – if I could have a shot of your pipe?'

'A shot?' Cliff took it from his mouth and examined it. 'Oh, you mean a go, a puff. Well, why not, although I think you'll find it very nasty.'

'I've always wanted to try a pipe.'

She clenched her teeth in Cliff's toothmarks on the damp yellow stem and inhaled scorching ashes, but refused to choke, although her eyes were watering.

'Nice,' she said handing it back.

'Come on then, girlie, let's go home for tea. A little bird told me that there will be scones and jam.'

'They will be horrid,' said Rowena, but she put her hand in the big hand Cliff was holding out to her.

The way he said 'scoanes' stood for everything that was wrong with this place. The piles of dirty washing, the scummy baths, the lopsided swing that always went round in a circle, the jam either running off the spoon or set solid and full of stones, so that you had to cut it with a knife, Wendy's turnip cake that wasn't fit for cows. Chestnuts was nothing like the boarding schools in books. Or the calm schoolroom at the Castle.

Rowena felt sad for Cliff, looking forward to his biscuity scoanes. She saw a batch of Aunt Mysie's scones cooling on a rack, light and high as a dozen chefs' hats. As they approached the house where, on what was once the lawn, a boy in feathered headdress and warpaint lay across the swing, kicking up clouds of dust with his bare feet, Rowena squared her shoulders. Cliff Waddilove felt the tremor in his arm, mistook it for acceptance of Chestnuts and squeezed her hand to show he understood. He started to sing 'There Was a Man Who Had a Horsalum'. Actually, Rowena had resolved that if she must stay here, she would at least teach Wendy Waddilove how to make scones. Then she remembered the fearsome Mrs Diggins from the village who ruled the kitchen.

'And, girlie, no more biting Heinz, eh? We don't bite each other at Chestnuts.'

Thereafter, the word 'girlie' would always evoke the pale pink ribbon in her hair that day, and 'a little bird told me' would send a little bird flying from the rim of a messy bowl of scone dough, to perch on Cliff Waddilove's shoulder and twitter in his ear.

The next day, Wendy, wearing her red-and-white

spotted scarf jauntily knotted, drove into town and came back with a box of clay pipes and all the Chestnuts staff and children spent the morning blowing soap bubbles. Sometimes a single bubble shimmered and expanded almost to shattering point before detaching itself, or hemispheres, each with a swirl of rainbow, piled one upon another in a brief airy construction. So Rowena's dream of flight burst, and there she sat on the grass, with her hair in a fringe that needed trimming, wearing the kilt she had arrived in, handed down from Hamish and now distinctly grubby, dipping her clay pipe into the soapy water, waving a stream of bubbles from its bowl, quite as if a cluster of iridescent globes on a summer breeze was ample compensation for everything that had been taken from her.

Chestnuts policy was to let the pupils discover the best in themselves; thus was Tilly Vernon who had burned down her previous school appointed Fire Monitor, and in the same spirit, Rowena, who had scowled dumbly when introduced to the Chestnuts poultry, was put in charge of the hens. They looked like the hard-faced women in headscarves who stand gossiping on street corners and make comments as you walk past. There was a terrifying cockerel called Mr Sunshine; Rowena renamed him Razor King. Egg production, or rather egg consumption, fell when she began aiding and abetting the hens who laid away.

It was decided that, although small for her age, Rowena should be upgraded to Candles. She disliked the Sticky Buds, with their jammy mouths and food-stained fronts, as much as the chickens. Sometimes when she was alone in the grounds she tried to pretend that she was Mary Lennox in *The Secret Garden*; she had come from India once and she felt sallow and contrary enough, but instead of a friendly robin, Cliff Waddilove kept bobbing up in her path in his brown tweed jacket and scarlet waistcoat.

During the Chestnuts time, Rowena longed for a room of her own. Later, she yearned for a community of souls, but although she had joined evening classes and attended bookshop readings and lectures in galleries, when they finished she was, as she had arrived, alone. 'I am waiting for my people to come for me,' was a thought that had sustained her over the years, and sometimes she almost believed that they would. Meanwhile, she was always a visitor, an observer through windows of other people's domestic interiors and, in her employment by various agencies as home help, cleaner and nurse, an auxiliary to other people's lives. Somewhere along the way she had lost her own; perhaps somebody else had found it and was living it. At her first sight of the Nautilus, it was if the lustre of the building filled her heart and ran through her veins.

She was dreaming of Cliff Waddilove conjuring a hen's egg from behind her ear, an egg that grew enormous. In the moment of waking she realised it was Gus's ostrich egg and the name Augustus Egg came to mind. The Victorian egg on its three-legged gilt stand and the Victorian artist. Gus had on that fur coat like a great borscht-coloured bear. Angus, in his HMS *Dunedin* hat, watches from the windowsill. Like a tribal fetish made from feathers, beads and bone, which has acquired genuine potency from its absorption of a people's hopes, fears and dreams, Angus, sole witness of Rowena's history, is more than a manufactured homunculus of celluloid and velvet.

3

Morning. Beads of condensation on the plumbing, tap water thudding into Rowena's galvanised bucket and Francis Campion's aluminium kettle, a smell of detergent and scrubbed wood, the Nautilus steaming in the bay as the sun dries a recent shower. Gus, carrying a large carton, passes Rowena on a stepladder in the hall; she is almost a silhouette against the subaqueous light of the window she is dusting with what looks like candyfloss on a long stick. Not wanting to startle her and cause her to fall, he goes out without saying good morning.

Celeste Zylberstein is sitting on the breakwater with her hands clasped on the parrot-headed stick Gus found for her, wearing an olive-coloured jacket with many pockets, matching trousers and a cotton hat. She has given up driving but her last car, the Wolsey, is still in the garage.

'Got your battledress on, I see,' says Gus. 'Off anywhere exciting?'

'To Croydon, for a show of solidarity with some Kosovan Albanian asylum seekers who are being quite disgracefully mistreated. Why don't you come with me, Gus? Add a bit of muscle? We need all the support we can get.'

'I've got a meeting at ten. You can borrow this if

you like.' He holds out the carton, a soap box marked Persil Biological. 'Don't get arrested. Oh, I almost forgot, here's the card of those decorators I was telling you about.'

Celeste glances at it and sees the name NATTERJACK and the logo of a toad with a yellow stripe down its back, before buttoning it into her breast pocket. Gus looks like a spiv this morning, with his hair slick from the shower and a cigarette in the side of his mouth, the black shirt which she hates and broad yellow tie, dark glasses with a swirl of iridescence on the lens. Gus is an enigma; she feels as though she knows him no better now than on the day he moved in. He comes, he goes; he smokes cannabis in his chamber and uses it as a stockroom; his eyes are hidden behind shades. There is a wife and family somewhere in the background.

Disappointed by his failure to a offer her a lift at least part of the way, she suppresses the thought that Gus Crabb is just a charming wide boy from Canvey Island on the make; she'd been touched by his story of a grandfather swept out to sea in a caravan by the floods of 1953. Had Gus forgotten that he had been homeless when she took him in?

Celeste loves the Essex coast and she had been intrigued to learn that Gus's mother was the daughter of Plotlanders, the people who had bought their marshy strips of real estate for a song and set up home there in hand-built shacks and old railway carriages, cultivating their gardens and constructing permanent dwellings. Communities of all sorts fascinated her, from the individualistic settlements of Plotlands and Dungeness to benevolent dictatorships and philanthropic democracies. Port Sunlight, Bourneville, Portmeirion, Hampstead Garden Suburb, Welwyn Garden City, Letchworth, all the new towns, Celeste and her husband Arkady had visited them, in pleasurable research for their own housing schemes.

Arkady had not lived to see the demolition of his last commission, a junior school in Croydon. Nor did he know that it had been a mercy killing, of a building first vandalised by the authorities, who had systematically felled its trees, tarmacadamed its grass, removed its drinking fountains and replaced its original glass. Celeste had chanced upon the school's destruction, and it was like a second funeral service for Arkady, in clouds of dust and ashes.

Arkady had been gone for more than twenty years now. He had collapsed at an architectural conference at the De La Warr Pavilion in Bexhill-on-Sea. To the paramedics, he was merely one more inconsiderate elderly tripper, but Celeste and Arkady had loved the building since its inception and numbered its architects, Erich Mendelsohn and Serge Chermayeff, among their friends.

Francis Campion as well as Gus is a broken reed these days, but what depresses her most is that the issues which really bring people on to the streets are their right to kill small animals, hit their children, buy cheap petrol and eat beef on the bone. Oh, but the chickens are coming home to roost.

'It is necessary only for the good man to do nothing for evil to triumph!' she calls after Gus.

Yeah, yeah. Better find yourself a good man then, thinks Gus, knotting the twine that holds the Ford Transit's doors closed. Who in their right mind would seek asylum in Croydon? Anyway, I've done my bit. Celeste had him trudging sheepishly round Crystal Palace Park last summer, trying to conceal the placard she'd thrust on him, in a march against the multiplex leisure complex that property developers, in cahoots with Bromley Council, still threatened to build there. A group of crusties had set up a protest camp and, until they'd finally been cherry-picked from the trees, Celeste had been at the park in all weathers, taking provisions of food, soap and cigarettes, like a superannuated Red Riding Hood with her scarlet anorak and basket of goodies. He'd stuck a poster of Joseph Paxton, architect of the Crystal Palace, with the caption SAVE MY PARK, in the shop window. What did she expect, blood? At the snap of a branch in the undergrowth Gus turns quickly as he climbs into the van. He hears giggling, the sound of running feet. He shrugs. Kids.

Crabb's Antiques suffers from its location, on a congested one-way system and between a restaurant which is always changing hands and cuisines, and a shop dealing in military insignia and memorabilia, ex-army surplus clothes and second-hand biker gear, specialist magazines and drugs. There is a tattoo parlour in the back and the proprietor, known to Gus as Urban Blight, does house clearances for the relatives of dead perverts. Currently, the restaurant is calling itself the Fragrant Thai but Gus could tell the Fragrant Thai that it will fail, like all its predecessors, because this parade of shops is built on one of the area's several plague pits. Or so he has come to believe.

Gus sets a raddled balloon-back chair on the pavement in the sun and lights a cigarette. He sees no reason not to since Urban has already lowered the tone by piling up all sorts of junk outside his premises, and it is unlikely that any customers will come anyway. From time to time, though, Gus strikes lucky and it's that which keeps him going and consoles him that he won't always be stuck in this dead-and-alive hole; it was at an auction of twentieth-century furniture that he'd met Celeste for the first time, and that had proved to be a lucky break.

It's a day to be at the seaside, not sitting here like two of eels, as his dad would say, in the traffic fumes. He'd like to be enjoying a pint outside the Crooked Billet at Old Leigh with Dad, like old times. He can see the view clearly; the wooden cockle shops, the looped stone and steel ribbon of the footbridge that links the levels, and across the estuary a dredger passing Canvey Island where the refinery towers are shimmering in a heat haze. Wild flowers and marram grasses are growing along the path between the railway line and the beach wall above the slope of what looks like volcanic tar that has melted and set again a thousand times, into the strip of beach that turns to swirls of mud shining almost to the horizon. An offshore breeze sets up a metallic clinking in the rigging of small boats and dinghies waiting for the tide to float them, and far out are silhouetted figures digging for shellfish or worms.

He had taken Lois there, because he was in that phase of infatuation where you want to show the beloved all your childhood haunts. A very bad idea, because it had rained and they'd run into his mum buying birthday cards in the Lynne Tait Gallery, and that was when the proverbial hit the fan.

He looks at his watch. How long to go before it's

time to drive to the school and park round the corner so he can watch the children come out?

At ten o'clock sharp, Rowena raps the shell on Francis Campion's door. These door knockers were designed to rotate, so that if a resident did not wish to be disturbed, to sport the oak as it were, the tip of the shell pointed down. Initially, Francis had been reluctant to avail himself of her services, declaring, 'We could certainly do with some general maintenance but I've shifted for myself all these years, thank you very much, and I see no reason to change now.'

Rowena had thought a change of shirt might be advisable, and what did that suggest of sheets? Yet, even if he had tied bits of wood to his feet, Francis was quite untainted by the lardy smell of the unwashed, exuding instead the faintest tang of clove and carnation. He was as papery as a disc of honesty. A zigzag blue vein had flickered ominously at his temple and Rowena was relieved to see it subside when they agreed that she would give his rooms a weekly going-over.

Francis ignores her tentative knock, although he was up and dressed early in anticipation of the invasion of his territory. He watched from his window Celeste setting out on some quest or deed of derring-do, some skiamachic errand, with her parrot-headed lance. His own conclusion that the human race is composed of evil children who will never grow up has released him from the obligation to engage further with the atrocities it commits in every corner of its wrecked playground.

Rowena's deferential tapping and the ensuing silence irritate him as much as a heartier knock would have done and makes her visit no less a disruption of his daily routine. He empties and refills his fountain pen, remembering that he'd woken with an idea which he'd lost in the time it took to pull up his blind, and reflects that cartoonists are spot-on in their depiction of thoughts enclosed in cloudy bubbles, that so quickly burst and drift away. A light bulb above his head flashes on, then, with a tinkling sound, the filament expires.

On the other side of the door, with the antiquated vacuum cleaner at her heels, nervous and with unfocused hopes, Rowena imagines herself handling books and scholarly papers reverently, and at the same time wants Francis to recognise her as a kindred spirit. This is the closest she's come to a poet in the flesh since she failed to get a job in the Poetry Society café.

She was once told that she does not have a first-class mind, but she is a grade A magpie, adept at snatching and secreting gaudy names and trinkets of ideas. Over the years she has amassed a cache of treasures, memorising poems with the thought that should she ever be placed in solitary confinement, she will not be quite alone. She was a fluent reader by the age of four and had the run of the Castle library as well as her aunt's books, but she left Chestnuts with, *inter alia*, a Woolworths autograph album, inscribed 'Be good, sweet maid, and let who will be clever!' and signed by Cliff with a sketch of a smoking pipe. Frequently, when attempting an article full of references that are beyond her, she comes upon a foreign word or phrase that is so beautiful and weighted with meaning that she feels she has absorbed the essence of the piece and need read no more. The name Celeste Zylberstein strikes chromatic notes of glockenspiel and zither from her nerves.

What is the old devil Francis Campion playing at? She knows he's in there, and that he knows she's outside. White campion, red campion, bladder campion. Thomas à Campion, no, à Kempis. Thomas Campion. Edmund Campion. Francis's ancestors? Metaphysical poets, detectives or martyrs? Better stick with the botanical, and see if any clues come up.

'Sparkle, Shirley, sparkle!' she murmurs as she catches sight of the name on the spray can of polish in the neat carrier, green plastic, divided by the handle into two compartments, where she keeps her cleaning equipment. Her mind's eye plays an exemplary clip from a TV documentary on child movie stars, featuring a reluctant moppet in a white dress all befrilled and flounced, who is hanging back shyly from making her entrance. 'Sparkle, Shirley, sparkle!' commands the tot's mother, encouraging her on stage with a brisk maternal shove, and dashing the tears from her baby-blues, golden ringlets bobbing professionally under an enormous bow, sparkle the tiny trouper does.

'It's Rowena,' she calls brightly, rapping the shell again.

The door opens, and the poet greets her with an exaggerated bow, flourishing his fountain pen, as if he has been interrupted mid-verse. He is wearing a frayed but freshly ironed green shirt and his hair is fluffed up like a dandelion clock.

'Ah, Rowena the Cleaner. Come in, come in.'

As she does, he sings, to the tune of 'Dinah', 'Roweena, is there anybody cleeaner, In the state of Caroleena?'

Seeing her affronted look, he says, 'Allow me to amend that ill-chosen comparative to Rowena the Clean-est.'

He takes in the print overall she is wearing, with a vaguely familiar hand-blocked pattern, and her hair, more Stephenson's Blue-Black than Waterman's Encre Noir, and the toolbox thing bristling with brushes, a can of Sparkle and virgin yellow dusters.

Quite unable to sparkle, Rowena realises that the pinafore is giving out the wrong signals. She found it in the kitchen cupboard, wrapped round an unfinished clay head that had long ago dried out. Gentle hand-washing revealed the colours of the print, but perhaps it has more of the skivvy than the artist about it. She sees herself trundling up to the Nautilus on the day she moved in, wheeling her suitcase and dragging the shopping trolley with a mop head sticking out, making deep ruts in the shingle and crunching so loudly that she expected a head to appear at every window; too many wheels skirring to a halt by the anchor, and too many of those blue plastic bags that smell of curry.

'I'd prefer it if you didn't address me like the chambermaid from Porlock,' she says. 'Mrs Zylberstein did invite me to be the Resident Housekeeper.'

'In point of fact, it was a democratic vote. We do everything here democratically, always have done. You should have seen us in our palmy days – the *Sturm und Drang*, the ideological wrangling. We even had a duel once.'

Rowena glimpses a palm-court orchestra playing Wagner in the Nautilus Bar, the flashing of swords.

'A duel? Was that over an ideological wrangle or an affair of the heart?'

He taps the side of his nose conspiratorially, and as Rowena looks in vain for a duelling scar, wondering if the duel had comprised pistols at dawn, her heartbeat quickens with the knowledge that any ideological wrangling would expose her utterly. The phrase 'dialetical materialism' flashes into her mind, representing all the things she has never looked up, that make her brain flinch like a jellyfish hit by a handful of pebbles.

'I daresay you'll have come across that cracked mirror behind the bar in the course of your duties,' Francis goes on. 'Happy days. I say, I don't suppose there's a chance that the Nautilus Bar might be restored to its former glory under your new regime? It's tragic to see it mouldering away, dry as the Sahara, a ghostly pianist tickling the ivories and the skeletons on the bar stools toasting absinthe friends.'

'You voted for me? When?'

When Gus had brought her to the Nautilus there had been no suggestion of any formal procedure. She was quaking as he led her to Francis and Celeste, reminding herself to sparkle. There they sat in the garden, like two chess pieces or a Henry Moore King and Queen.

'While Gus was showing you the studios. Carried unanimously. *Nem. con.* Ms Rowena Snow was generally considered to be an asset to the Nautilus community.'

At the word 'community', Rowena's embarrassment at the thought of being discussed is tempered by the knowledge that she was elected by people who not only knew how to pronounce names like Henri Gaudier-Brzeska, László Moholy-Nagy and Mies van der Rohe, but had probably met their owners. Long ago, she had memorised the names of *Les Six*, perhaps in anticipation of some future test, and she saw that her study might pay off soon. 'What music do you like?' Celeste would ask, happening on Rowena riffling through the 78s in their brittle paper sleeves. Have you any Germaine Tailleferre?' comes the casual reply.

'You've got a beautiful smile. You should use it more often.'

Rowena frowns, to nip in the bud any hint of flirtation, knowing from experience how it can develop into a poisonous flower. She should have said Celeste, not Mrs Zylberstein. Had she even accidentally pronounced it Zylberstien?

'So – Francis – what would you like me to do?'

Her glance ranges round the clutter obscuring the curves of the chamber's design, piles of books and broken accordion files spilling sheets of manuscript, documents and newspapers, a postcard of a puffin and four oak apples in a glass of dirty water, taking in the spines of books stamped with the Paper Nautilus shell and names, Francis Campion apart, mostly unknown. What joy he must get every day from seeing his books, how proud of them he must be. She is holding as a treat in reserve the exploration of the great printing press.

A badly made bed looms. The nicotined walls cry out for Manger's Sugar Soap. She should have brought up the long-handled duster, but rather than make herself late by stopping to remove the spiders' sticky nets and dead flies, she had left it in the garden. She could have run down to fetch it several times while he'd kept her waiting. 'Oh, you won't find much to occupy yourself here, as I said. I've always kept the place as clean as a whistle, clean as a milk thistle.'

Rowena, dispirited again by the lumpy quilt trailing a swag of sheet to the floor, the pills that remind her that both Francis and Celeste are potential candidates for nursing care, stares. It is one thing to speak of affairs of the heart with a distinguished poet, to whom rhyming must come as naturally as breathing, quite another to be patronised by an old loony, and she hasn't failed to notice that his kettle, whistle and all, is seriously lime-scaled. All the vitreous baths, sinks and basins of the Nautilus resemble bottle glass which has been roughened and clouded by the sea. The water-softening unit itself has been calcified by the hard London water. The scenario is all too reminiscent of her last position. Shades of Pipe-Cleaner Man, who lost her her job with the Caring Options Agency. Perhaps she has set herself a hopeless task in bringing order to the Nautilus. The seven maids with seven mops syndrome. The Augean stables. Her arms start to itch, as if she is wearing scratchy wool, although they are bare beneath short cotton sleeves. The invisible itchy jumper she brought from Chestnuts still brings her skin out in welts at times of stress.

Francis doesn't know why he said 'milk thistle' but it brings Magnus Scrabster's silky locks to mind. If he hadn't used up all the milk, he could ask Rowena to make coffee. Then he remembers seeing the name Milk Thistle on a bottle of tablets in Superdrug when he'd been looking for a sponge.

Rowena visibly pulls herself together, folds her arms and straightens her back. There is a green spiral-bound notebook on the desk, with *Take Me Back to the Gaierty Hotel* written on a white label stuck to its cover. Presumably work in progress. His autobiography? Mr Salteena in *The Young Visiters*. Aunt Mysie's copy had marbled endpapers and a frontispiece photograph of the youthful author; little Rowena had envied Daisy Ashford her golden hair and the sailor suit she wore.

Wondering what lost gaierty Francis Campion yearns for, and suppressing her impulse to identify the quote, she says, brisk but sensitive, 'I take it the desk's a no-go area. I think I'll make a start on hoovering the available floor space. Has the carpet always been that colour?'

'Probably not. At least give a thought to opening up the bar in due course.'

'It would have to be put to a vote,' says Rowena. 'Anyway, there are so few residents now, I don't think it would be viable. I mean, it's not like the palmy days, is it, with the *Sturm und Drang* and all the crowned heads of Bohemia flocking to SE19? And besides, I'm not a barmaid.'

Although she has seen two palm trees, a bit raggedy and moth-eaten, in the grounds.

'Another thing, this vacuum cleaner – it must be the one Noah used in the ark.'

'Mrs Noah, I daresay,' Francis agrees, adding, 'Have a word with Mr Fixit, he'll pick one up for you cheap.'

'Mr Fixit?' Was there some handyman of whom she'd been unaware, malevolently skulking in the basement as she blithely invaded his territory? Like the bogeyman who lived behind the Chestnuts boiler, hideously festooned with grey cobwebs.

'Jonathan Jo with a mouth like an O and a wheelbarrow full of surprises. Gus. You name it, he'll get it for you.'

'But I was thinking of something state-of-the-art. Twenty-first century rather than state-of-dead-person's-house-clearance-art. A bit Bauhaus. Something with a bit of oomph.' It is the first time she has spoken the word *Bauhaus* aloud and she is gratified by the natural way it fell into the conversation. It's just a shame Celeste wasn't present.

As she negotiates books and files and approaches the door, Rowena realises that Francis is trying to communicate something to her through the roaring of the vacuum cleaner. She switches off and straightens up, feeling as if two vertebrae have fused.

'Mind the hat!' he is saying as the noise subsides in a resentful wheeze. 'Don't knock down the hat.'

He points to the Homburg, is it, on the back of the door. 'That's Louis MacNeice's hat.'

'What? That's Louis MacNeice's hat? Really?'

'Yes, yes. I'd rather it wasn't sucked into that thing you're wielding with such gay abandon,' he says, more than a little miffed by the way her whole face has lit up.

'May I touch it?'

He shrugs, and Rowena strokes the greying pile with a finger and sees, beneath the band where a stitch or two have rotted, the original coal black of the material, bright as the day when Louis MacNeice wore it home from the hatter's.

Francis waits for her to lift the hat from the peg, to examine the interior for traces of the poet's hair oil, or an undiscovered poem, to put it on, run into the bathroom and flirt with herself in the glass above the basin and, expecting him to share her amusement at how much too large it is for her little head, to push it back and strut about like a gangster. She merely places the side of her hand in the valley between grey hills and rests it there for a moment.

'Did he give it to you? Or leave it here by mistake?'

'We exchanged hats,' said Francis.

Rowena imagines the two poets in a field. With a ceremonious bowing of heads, each removes and hands the other his black hat as a mark of respect, like football captains exchanging shirts after a glorious contest.

Eventually, she packs her duster and the can of Sparkle.

'Well, thank you,' she says.

'*Au contraire*, thank *you*.'

He holds the door open for her and watches her disappear round the sweep of the passage, the vacuum cleaner getting a wheel tangled up in its own flex and going belly-up like a stranded dugong.

'"Come back early or never come,"' he calls after her.

The dugong is dragged out of sight, leaving Francis wondering as he closes his door. He judges Rowena to inhabit a volatile emotional climate with rapidly changing weather. Sunshine and showers. Whacking great chip on her dusky shoulder, though. He suspects that she has never been married. A solitary lass. Naturally, she was discreet at her interview but perhaps time would tell; one doesn't turn up with one's past neatly folded in a single suitcase, to be unpacked, the creases shaken out and hung up systematically; the past comes crumpled in an assortment of carrier bags too, which might never be taken out of the darkest recess of the wardrobe where they were stowed on arrival. A dreadful thought seizes him. What if she has a stash of unpublished poems? He should have seen it before, that fringe, the febrile reaction to the hat. Unquestionably, Rowena Snow is a poetess in disguise.

Out of sight, Rowena stops suddenly, as if hit on the back of the head by an egg. Of course Ms Snow was voted an asset to the Nautilus, she's a bloody cleaner, isn't she? She recalls Gus walking past her without a word and her happiness at Francis calling the MacNeice refrain after her vanishes. She is glad she'd decided to ignore the bed even though it goes against the grain to leave a sheet with unmitred corners. Gus was the last person she'd consult about a new vacuum cleaner. Had she done or said anything to offend him? Well, she sure wasn't going to hover round him, be kept waiting outside his door to find out. She had come to the Nautilus with the determination never to live in someone else's time again. Palmy days. Celeste and Francis are two ancient palm trees and she is the monkey sent running up for coconuts.

But then she remembered how, on the day after she had moved in, Celeste took her into the library at the heart of the shell. Sunshine was filtering through the opaque glass dome on to circle after circle of bookshelves.

'It's wonderful, even better than the Reading Room at the British Museum!'

Celeste touched a button and one bookstack ran back on a curved steel rail to reveal yet more books behind. Rowena's eyes filled with tears and with blurred double vision she saw thousands of books, periodicals, learned journals, magazines and pamphlets, all the knowledge in the world spiralling around her. Celeste sat down on a set of library steps and pulled out a volume of drawings, blowing the dust off before turning the pages as Rowena ranged the library. A green padded bench, wide enough to lie on, ran round the walls, a massive desk of the colour and texture of polished driftwood stood at the centre, and chairs, some egg-shaped and others which were single slices of wood bent into a variety of attitudes from sitting to lounging, were dotted about. Artificial lighting was provided by large glass pearls on the walls and free-standing anglepoise-type lamps whose shades were aluminium scallop shells. Underneath some of the bookshelves were sliding racks of prints and technical drawings that glided out on silken runners, and there were two globes on the desk, one showing the earth and the other the heavens.

'I suppose I should start at the top,' Rowena said.

'What, and read your way downwards?'

'I meant dusting them and cleaning the shelves.'

'Why don't you just dust each one as you read it?' Celeste suggested. 'I'd much rather you enjoyed the library. It's been neglected for too long.'

Overawed by choice, Rowena hovered in front of rows of green and yellowed-white Penguins. What she really felt like doing was curling up in an enormous green egg with a good detective story. Celeste seemed engrossed in her tome, so that was what she did. It was the happiest afternoon she had spent since her aunt died.

Until he heard himself boasting of it to Rowena, Francis had quite forgotten about the long-ago duel that wrecked the Nautilus Bar. It is all coming back to him now, emerging from the mists of memory, the smog of 1952, to be precise.

That winter, as Londoners stoked up their coal fires against the cold, a blanket of warmer air trapped the smoke from millions of chimneys until, by the fatal chemistry that created, they were actually breathing in droplets of sulphuric acid. Francis remembers buses crawling along the roads, guided by their conductors carrying torches and lamps. Those who could stay indoors did, as the yellow poison tried to sneak into the Nautilus; while the doors and windows were closed, the building was as tightly sealed as a submarine. News filtered through that the hospitals were full of people dying, that two coaches had crashed in Croydon, even that thieves and murderers were taking advantage of days turned to night. It seemed to Francis as he groped his way to and from Broadcasting House that the smog was both an evil presence in itself and a cloak beneath which emanations of the underworld, the drains, sewers and secret rivers beneath the city, slithered upwards through gratings and manholes with wicked intent.

At that time, all the chambers of the Nautilus were occupied. As well as Francis himself, Celeste and Arkady and their children Konstantin and Susannah, among the residents were a volatile couple known, in a slur on that breed's good name, as the Bedlington Terriers. Irina Bedlington-Turner was an actress who had enjoyed a recent *succès d'estime* in her own adaptation of Gertrude Stein's *Tender Buttons*. She was presently rehearsing a series of dramatic monologues, with incidental jazz and female chorus, spoken by the widows of fishermen lost at sea. Her husband Bob, a tallow-faced, drooping moustached, six-footer who claimed an obscure Bloomsbury connection, was a painter. Periodically, one or other of them destroyed his canvases. The couple's fights were legendary, often beginning in Soho drinking clubs and continuing in the Nautilus Bar. At last, their behaviour had necessitated an Extraordinary Meeting of the Democratic Council. The resident barman, Paul, a violinist in the Nautilus string ensemble, had cut his hand while sweeping up the broken glass after one of their quarrels and was threatening to pack his bags. Margot the cook, insulted beyond endurance by cigarettes stubbed out in untasted food, had barred them from the dining room. Irina and Bob were bound over for good behaviour, on pain of expulsion.

During the following three months, all had been quiet on the Bedlington Terrier front, but now the term of their probation was over and the community was watching them with some anxiety. Francis had reason to avoid them both; he disliked Bob intensely and Irina was pestering him for advice about her work-in-progress. He was not flattered. Her motives were transparent; she was hoping he would use his influence at the Third Programme to get the monologues broadcast, starring, of course, herself. Even when she was on the wagon, Francis found Irina's intensity alarming. With its cap of glossy black hair like fresh paint, her porcelain skin, green eyes and scarlet cupid's-bow mouth, her face reminded him of one of those Pierrot wall plaques which were fashionable in the thirties.

The smog was its worst on the night Francis arrived home, cold and hungry, exhausted by the journey which had taken three hours. The dirty yellow vapour clung to his overcoat and hat and had penetrated the scarf wound round his mouth and nose. He could feel it clogging his throat and lungs. Music was coming from the bar and, attracted by the thought of warmth and company, a mellow whisky to wash away the taste of the fog, Francis decided to go straight there. Several people were grouped at tables in the marine light; Arkady was at the piano, Celeste on a stool at the bar.

Francis was walking over to join her, when a flying missile struck him hard in the face. Then Bob Bedlington Terrier had him by the throat and was beating him about the head. Francis was on the floor, shielding his face with his arms.

'How do you account for this?' Bob kicked him in the ribs and waved the weapon, one of Francis's wooden slats, in front of him, shouting, 'Explain what your shoes were doing under my wife's bed!'

Celeste and Arkady now had Bob by his arms. Irina was flailing at her husband with the other slat.

'*I* can explain, you fool! It's nothing to do with Francis! Leave him, Bob. You're drunk. You'll get us thrown out.'

But Bob broke free from Arkady and Celeste, pushed Irina aside and struck Francis across the face with the slat. He grabbed the other shoe from Irina and threw it at Francis.

'You have dishonoured my wife. I challenge you to defend yourself!'

Francis, with blood pouring down his face, got painfully to his feet, picked up the slat and rushed at Bob. They fought their way round the bar, ignoring screams, knocking over chairs and stools. Francis was in total confusion as to why he had been accused, but was powered by rage and hatred.

Bob had jumped up on to the bar and was throwing

bottles. Paul got him by the legs and he toppled. Francis felt himself pinioned, as he hurled his weapon with all his force at Bob's head. It struck the mirror behind the bar with a splintering crack.

In the morning Irina, sobbing, came to Francis's chamber to apologise. She winced at the sight of his two black eyes, under the bandage on his forehead, and the cut across the bridge of his nose. 'Your poor, handsome face. I can't bear it to be so wounded.' She confessed that she had taken his fisherman's shoes. 'I was blocked,' she said. 'I had the idea that if I put on your shoes while I was writing, they might inspire me. I thought that the drowned voices of fisherfolk might speak to me through them. I see now that I was making a sort of subliminal association of soles and souls. But actually, I have to admit, I was hoping that some of your genius might rub off on me.'

She looked up at him, her green eyes brimming over again. Francis handed her a handkerchief, but he knew that her tears sprang not from remorse but the fear she had put paid to her chances with the BBC.

A few days later, the Bedlington Terriers, united in disgrace, were escorted from the premises. The smog had cleared and the small crowd which had assembled could see clearly the rude hand gestures coming from the windows of the van loaded with their possessions.

It was decided that the crack in the mirror should not be repaired but would be preserved as a permanent warning against intemperance. As far as Francis knew the monologues had never been performed.

4

When Celeste arrives at Lunar House, the Home Office headquarters of the Immigration and Nationality Directive, the reflective-striped yellow jackets of the police suggest that today's demonstration might have attracted more people than the small permanent cluster of protesters there but, disappointingly, the police outnumber the demonstrators. The turnout is just big enough to irritate the shoppers heading for the underpass to the Whitgift Centre. The public frenzy, whipped up by the tabloids and endorsed by politicians, against so-called Bogus Asylum Seekers – the term suggests to Celeste an army of ghosts, spectral bands of gypsies trudging over Eastern Europe – has died down, at least here in London, where fear of violence has caused the women begging with their children to vanish from the streets. Now paedophiles, real or falsely accused, are the flavour of the month and the target of vigilante mobs. Outside Lunar House, supplicants of various nationalities stand or crouch, supported by handmade placards pasted with photocopied documents and photographs. Every picture tells a story but nobody pauses to read. Inside, some fifteen miles of shelving sag beneath the weight of 200,000 case files bulging with a backlog of heartbreak, lies and truths lost in the translation.

Celeste greets one or two campaigners, then sees a woman bearing down on her, whose face, framed by an aureole of grey hair, is transparent with relief at spotting another middle-class Englishwoman. She is wearing, perhaps to show solidarity, a quasi-peasant outfit of ethnic skirt, embroidered blouse and sandals, and slung from her shoulder is a large holdall with rope handles.

'This is getting to be a habit with me,' she smiles. 'Protesting in Croydon, I mean. I was part of the Boycott Nestlé contingent,' she explains. 'Not that I'm local. I've got a friend, a distinguished artist actually, who lives not too far away, and it's easy to get here from her house.'

I don't want to know any of this, thinks Celeste. 'You sound quite the professional,' she smiles back. Distinguished artist my eye.

'Oh, I wouldn't put it quite like that. One does what one can. But – well,' she hesitates, then goes on in a rush of confidence, 'I don't know about you, but somehow one never feels quite at the heart of it. One never seems to actually get to *know* anybody at these affairs. They can be awfully cliquey, can't they?'

'There *can* be a language barrier sometimes.'

'I wonder if this town ever *will* be granted city status? It is of a hideousness, and soullessness, don't you agree? They'd be better off bulldozing the lot, in my opinion.'

'There are a lot of worthwhile buildings if you know where, and how, to look.'

'Oh, the Archbishop's Palace, I daresay, and the Clocktower, although I haven't managed to get to any of their art exhibitions – and Allders and Debenhams are still flying the flag, by and large, but Grants, that lovely old department store left to rack and ruin, and I'm not even sure how environmentally friendly the trams actually are.'

She plucks, like a drink from a passing waiter's tray at a party, a bunch of leaflets from a man's hand. 'Hang on, I haven't signed your petition yet,' she tells him, scrawling her name and leaving blank the space for the address.

'Sad though, when you think that Croydon derives from the Anglo-Saxon, *Crogden*, meaning Saffron Valley and that there were once fields of lavender all round these parts.'

'I think you'll find that's *Crogedene*, and I understand that Grants is to be restored, preserving the original façade. Are you involved in the Crystal Palace Campaign?' Celeste, playing the veteran, is determined not be out-leafleted or local-historied by a heritage upstart.

'Sadly, no. Well, I suppose I must brave the Whitgift. I'm on a mission to find a lemon reamer for an agoraphobic neighbour.'

The woman puts down her bag, pulls out a folded silver scooter and in one deft movement assembles and mounts it, scoots down the ramp to the underpass with the wind billowing her skirt and a backwards wave over her shoulder. Ridiculous at her age, and risking the overdevelopment of one calf muscle. Bonkers. A protest tourist. Yet Celeste is excited by a pang of envy. She wants that scooter.

She sits down to rest on a wall, troubled by the knowledge that, unknown to the comrades with whom she has been standing, not precisely shoulder to shoulder because she is shrinking with each passing year, she will go home to a building where her hypocrisy roars in the vacant chambers like the sea in an empty shell.

She contemplates walking to Turtle's emporium where she's sure to find something she needs, or taking a ride on one of the new trams. Tramlink is up and running, with the mayoral seal of approval, after years of debate and the town centre like a building site, but tramlines run backwards in her memory to converge at the vanishing point and these trams that travel through green and leafy tunnels cannot take her anywhere she wants to be. Lodz, Berlin, Hamburg, Paris, Cracow, Moscow; Wimbledon, New Addington, Elmers End.

If she'd been a few decades younger she could have pushed that girl in the big sandals off her scooter and wrested the handlebars from her grasp. Sighing, and leaning on her stick with its painted feathers and shrewd glass eyes, she pulls herself to her feet and makes for Marks and Spencer's food hall. How sad it is that at the Nautilus they have got into the habit of eating alone. They have become a boil-in-the-bag and microwave community. There will be no pleasure in whatever delicacies she buys.

Celeste had intended to travel home before the schoolchildren got out but she sees to her dismay a group of black blazers as she approaches the bus stop. Either she has lingered too long in Marks or some of them have escaped. She prays that the bus will come before the rest swarm on to the pavement. A bus, not the 468 Celeste wants, takes everybody else waiting at the stop, so that only she and five or six teenage schoolboys are left. Celeste is aware of something going on among them, studiously ignores them, then senses that the snorts and sniggers are directed at her. She looks up involuntarily and sees one of the boys unzipping his trousers. An enormous pink penis leaps out, flaunting itself. Shocked and enraged, Celeste shakes her stick at it, in contempt and refusal to be intimidated. She doesn't mean to strike the thing but, to her horror, the tip of her stick hooks it, and, as the boy yells, tosses it into the road. Paralysed, her stick still pointing at arm's length, she stares at the obscenely pink member curled in the gutter. The boys are laughing hysterically as the mutilated owner bends down and picks it up, stuffing it into his blazer pocket. Then God sends a 468 bus.

Celeste boards shakily, leaving the boys at the bus stop, and sits down, still trembling at the enormity of the deed she thought for a moment she had done, reliving the incident, when blood gushed and an ambulance flashed in her mind's eye. Only as the bus pulls away does she realise that, although the group was mixed, the perpetrator was black. She looks out of the window; the boys are still laughing, punching each other in mirth, prolonging their amusement. She smiles too then, weakly. Imagine being taken in by such an obvious trick. It was too big, too pink to be true. She gives the boys a little wave, as if she was in on the joke all along.

When she gets home she sits on a bench in dappled sunshine watching peacock butterflies on a white buddleia and further away the gibbons' arms of the monkey puzzle tree curving against the blue sky. She wipes her stick on a tussock of sea pinks, as if it has been dirtied by contact with that monstrosity. It was a pretty frightful thing to do to an old woman, she thinks. Such total lack of respect. A shock like that could have the most dreadful effect on somebody less tough than herself, or on a young girl. What if they jumped out on a woman in a dark street? Where had they procured such an object? A joke shop? A sex shop? She just wants to forget the incident, yet wonders if it is her embarrassing duty to ring their head teacher before somebody has a heart attack, and the mob scene from *Germinal*, which has been threatening at the back of her mind, thrusts into hideous focus a ragged lump of flesh trampled by the crowd.

Then she notices a spicy, fragrant scent that isn't coming from the M&S bag beside her on the bench, a wafting redolence of ginger and chillies, onions, tomatoes, garlic, coriander. The rich, red aroma with hints of green and yellow brings tears to her eyes. Somebody is cooking in the Nautilus kitchen.

Am I doing the right thing, Rowena worries in the saffron-scented steam, among the clashing, newly scoured, great steel and copper saucepans of her galley, or am I merely currying favour? If so, they will surely sniff my motive out, with contempt and pity. Her heart is racing, her hands are shaky. She is cooking, for the first time, a meal to which everybody will be welcome. The glazing onions, the tiny bubbles in red juice are like something; what is it, what is it, a length of scarlet silk, gold mesh, beaded gauze? It's gone.

Am I really here, in this kitchen, preparing this meal, or am I a child playing at cooking and dressing-up, she wonders, or am I in bed at Formosa Road, dreaming all this? She has on a chef's coat of stiff white cotton with a persistent stipple of mildew on the collar, and rusty imprints of lost metal buttons. If her mind could grasp that flash of scarlet and gold, would it take her back in time, and let her glimpse herself, as she was, before she became the child she remembered, kneeling up on a stool, wrapped in her aunt's apron, stirring something in a creamware mixing bowl with a wooden spoon that she had to grip in both hands? Is she still, *mutatis mutandis*, that little girl, or even the resentful teenager who'd hacked frozen mud from a heap of swedes in the Chestnuts kitchen?

Then memory exhales a purple whiff of methylated spirit, conjuring up a toy tin stove her aunt had bought her. It had sharp edges and got red-hot when you lit the spirit-soaked cotton wool in the burners. The pale green and cream paint of the stove bubbled into blisters, the handles of the cooking pots glowed. There were two saucepans which took a single diced potato or a few pods of peas. You could cut or burn your fingers, set your hair on fire. A lovely, dangerous toy. It would not be allowed these days, of course, and she would never have dreamed of giving such a thing to Iris Dunlop. A doll-sized canteen of cutlery; metal knives, forks and spoons, a tea set with green-painted tin cups that scalded your lips. Piece by piece, it comes back to her, each item in its special slot in the cardboard box with the picture of beaming kiddies on the lid; and now a long-forgotten humming top is spinning its painted merry-go-rounds into merging bands of colour, spiralling faster and faster until all colour is spun away.

She remembers a parcel arriving at Chestnuts, blobbed with red sealing wax and addressed in Lady Ferguson's writing. It contained a jigsaw puzzle of a map of

Scotland. Lady Ferguson became Lady Grouseclaw the day she packed Rowena off to Chestnuts. Until then Rowena loved her, and had even stroked the pheasants' feathers trembling on her hats, the foxes' paws that clasped her neck, the brooches made from birds' feet set with amethysts and tourmaline. From the bitter perspective of Chestnuts, the Castle bristled with rods, guns, traps and snares, the kitchen table was heaped with carcasses and an ashet full of blood stood on the draining board, birds hung in bunches from hooks and antlered heads mourned from the walls.

When Hamish wrote to her from his boarding school, she tore the letter into tiny pieces and scattered it in confetti over the Chestnuts chicken run. The hens rushed to peck, toss aside and trample the disappointing crumbs. Watching them, Rowena vowed never to think about Hamish ever again, or his big brothers who galloped her, shrieking, on their backs down the long corridors in the holidays, or any of the people who worked at the Castle, and specially not Lord Killdeer and Lady Grouseclaw. She hadn't even said goodbye to the dogs and she knew that nobody would explain why she didn't come to play with them any more.

Well, maybe Hamish did tell them, and the half-wild cats and the farm animals, when he came home, Rowena thinks now, as she cooks. Cautiously, she allows herself to remember a stocky boy with green eyes and thick fair hair, full of bravado about going away to school. His face zooms into sharp focus. 'Ohh.' The sound comes out as she doubles up in pain, as if from a blow to the stomach, at his white skin, the mole under his left eye. Rowena sits down, astonished that she has been carrying this picture of Hamish with her through the years, a tiny coloured photograph sealed into a cell in the honeycomb of her brain, and she doesn't know why she has found it today, in the Nautilus kitchen.

Graeme and Colin: the names of Hamish's brothers come to her. She wonders how Lord Killdeer and Lady Grouseclaw would have reacted if she and Hamish had eventually married as they'd planned; would they have smiled as indulgently at a dark daughter-in-law from a tied cottage as they had at two children paddling in the burn, and would Lord Killdeer have sung 'Ho ro my nut-brown maiden' so cheerily at the wedding reception as he did when he dandled her on his knee? Once she had imagined Hamish and herself living in the Castle, but she recognises that Graeme would have inherited it, Graeme's children ridden the rocking horse in the nursery and climbed the ladder to tie the star to the tip of the Christmas tree so tall that it took four men to drag it into the hall. What destiny had awaited Hamish, the youngest, landless son? She had hidden his letter from prying eyes, tucking it up the sleeve of her cardigan at breakfast before running down to the chicken coops, but what risks had Hamish himself taken in writing and posting it?

She can't remember if she ever wrote to thank Lady Grouseclaw for the presents she sent to Chestnuts. They stopped coming after a while. A match flares in burning cotton wool; green tin plates balanced on the long grass topple, spilling their blackberries and dolly mixtures. Ach, get on with your work, woman, sitting here moping over a lost jigsaw puzzle, a humming top in the Chad Valley of the Shadow and a prelapsarian tea set.

Rowena is terrified about the protocol for summoning the Nautilans to supper, and she imagines the white coat's original owner, tall, skinny, topped with a chef's hat, his cheeks puffed out like a Triton's as he blows into a conch to bring them crowding in from chamber, studio and garden. Or had he banged a gong, perhaps shaped like a dolphin? She couldn't do that, even if there was such a thing, too embarrassing, as if she were the landlady of a boarding house decked with seaside whimsy; here all the shells are austere and practical. And communal dining was always optional. She must rely on her fellow residents' olfactory nerves and let them exercise their right to choice, as she is doing in preparing this meal. Nobody suggested that her duties included cooking. Perhaps she would have to eat it all in solitary splendour. Smarty Arty had a party. No one came. Smarty Arty had another. Just the same. Fool not to have done it sooner – she switches on the radio to drown her eternal interior monologue, but not before Cliff Waddilove materialises on the front steps of Chestnuts, tooting on a toy bugle 'Come to the cookhouse door, boys, come to the cookhouse door' into the dusk.

This kitchen, the glass sinks, all these surfaces and utensils, all hers. A song tries to rise in Rowena's throat, but what should she sing? Mrs Diggins from the village, the cook at Chestnuts, would have killed for the knife block, the KitchenAid, the Waring Blender, the orange juicer, the Dualit toaster, the refrigerator and dishwasher. Mrs Diggins managed somehow to get a brown skin on everything she cooked in her industrial-sized aluminium vats, custard, stew, mashed potato, and all her greens were grey. As midday approached, the smell of her dinners swirled round Rowena's empty stomach in a queasy blend of hunger and nausea. Mrs Diggins first strode into her view, gaunt in a belted gabardine raincoat and short wellingtons, grasping in each hand a flapping hen by its legs, upside down. She had the face of a cruel spoon, and although she cracked dissident children on the head with her ladle, the received wisdom was that Mrs Diggins was a sport.

She had her favourites, girls who clung to her arms like counterweights in the bitter wind as she lumbered across the icy grass in her zip-fronted snowboots to join in a skipping game, or link arms with the gang chanting, 'Who wants to play – Cowboys and Indibums?' or declare:

'I am a Girl Guide dressed in blue,
These are the actions I can do:
Salute to the King
Salute to the Queen
Salute to the German submarine!'

At 'German submarine', Mrs Diggins thumbed her nose, and sometimes her bottom. The little girls squealed. Even Trudl, who, with Heinz and Ulrich, was always served last at dinner; sometimes there was no pudding left when it came to their turn. Trudl was not a Girl Guide: the Chestnuts children were barred from all the village's youth organizations.

She clapped together for warmth her big fur paws made from the skins of her own rabbits; favoured pupils nuzzled these gloves with their cold noses and stroked them. To be out of favour with Mrs Diggins was a state even the Waddiloves dreaded. Her umbrage was terrible. 'I've got the 'ump!' she would declare periodically and then fear stalked the school. 'Mrs

Diggins has got the 'ump! *Sauve qui peut!*' Cliff would whisper, and flee to hide in his study.

Even though some had the full complement of parents, Mrs Diggins bore tales of 'them poor little orphans' to the village, a terrifying place where the local children threw stones at the Chestnuts children and the shopkeepers despised them as refugees and accused them of stealing. They watched them like hawks, so that it was difficult to get away with even a halfpenny chew. How the village had sneered at the Chestnuts children's harvest festival gifts, ragged bunches of wild flowers and hand-made baskets filled with ripe conkers; the vicar placed them out of sight behind a pyramid of vegetable marrows. The Chestnuts ethos of self-expression was generally decried; it was bad enough that the pupils called their teachers by their Christian names, but when the Chestnuts handbell team took part in the All-Village Concert, not only were some of the band wearing lipstick but the pretty one in a pair of Mrs Waddilove's cast-off peep-toe shoes was obviously a boy.

Mrs Diggins wore a maroon-coloured lipstick which stained her cigarettes and the rim of her special teacup; in summer her stockings were rolled to the knee, under her flowered overall. She had a brooch in the shape of a spider with a purple glass belly, which was odd because she was always splatting insects and stubbing out cheesybugs with the toe of her boot. Bees and wasps drove her into a frenzy and a mouse in a trap always put her in a good mood. More often than not though, the children sprang the traps themselves and ate the cheese and bacon rinds.

Mrs Diggins had a daughter, Belinda, who was the

same age as Rowena. Once, as a special treat for the Chestnuts children, Belinda Diggins came to show them her bridesmaid's dress and the charm bracelet and locket which were a present from the bridegroom. She'd had her hair permed for the wedding.

So what song, all these years on, should Rowena sing? One of Cliff's surreal numbers with a rollicking chorus? He delighted in songs like 'Michael Finnegan', 'Green Broom', 'Twanky dillo, twanky dillo, twanky dillo dillo dillo, with a roaring pair of bagpipes while the boy works the bellows', or, 'with a wing wang waddle-o, Jack sold his saddle-o, blossy boys bubble-o, under the broom', and so on, hoping perhaps that singing in unison this archaic doggerel would make sense for these dispossessed children of a world which had made a nonsense of their lives. 'There was a man who had a horsalum,' Rowena sings now in his memory. 'Here we sit like birds in the wilderness, birds in the wilderness, birds in the wilderness. Here we sit like birds in the wilderness, down in Demerara.'

She need not have worried. There they all sit, unsummoned, unfolding their napkins which are crackingly clean but, like her chef's coat, spotted with the mildew which she is determined to eradicate. The table is set with a dinner service of graphite-coloured pottery feathered by red and yellow leaves, two steaming tureens at its centre. Gus is rolling up the sleeves of his black shirt in a businesslike way. He has removed his yellow tie and smells of citrus and spice cologne.

Rowena has changed into a black silky dress with a pattern of tiny white fans and a draped bodice which gives it a forties look; but will it suggest that she thinks this meal is a really big deal, even that she's trying to look like one of the original Nautilans? She decides to wear it round the place while she's working, just in case.

'What a charming dress,' says Francis.

'Oh, it's just a workaday frock.' She blushes, managing not to blurt out that it's 100 per cent viscose, £14.99 from Charisma of Norwood. Anyway, Celeste is wearing a scarf painted with peacocks' tails which pick up the colours of her earrings and the violet shadows round her eyes. But then, Celeste is never less than elegant and couldn't look scruffy if she tried. She has a black knitted silk jacket hanging off her shoulders, a look Rowena admires for its confidence that the garment won't slide to the floor, and she wonders if she might aspire to it herself some day.

'Thank you.' Rowena remembers that one must always take a compliment gracefully. Sparkle, Shirley, sparkle. Oh, why do I care so much what they think of me? I've *got* to cultivate casualness. Celeste is smiling at her. Her eyes are the colour of topaz.

'I can't tell you, my dear, how happy this makes me. All of us sitting together like this. Like the old days . . . like civilised beings.'

Ghosts are slouching in the shadows and pulling up the spare chairs which Rowena has lined against the walls.

'Well, I'm as hungry as a wolf,' says Francis. As a wolf in sheep's clothing; a lambswool pullover the colour of tinned salmon and knitted heather-mauve socks and his fisherman's slats. 'The Shoes of the Fisherman,' he explains when he notices Rowena looking at them. 'Had 'em for seventy-odd years. I was wearing them the night the Crystal Palace burned down, and when Croydon was bombed. Remember, Celeste?'

'Yes, I remember it well.' His words evoke pyrotechnics but her mind is on the vegetable plot that once supplied their table, now disappeared under brambles, and the senescent fruit trees, and the little swimming pool, full of leaves, that everyone's forgotten about. Suddenly she remembers another incident, which almost ended in tragedy.

'Those slats got you into serious trouble once, if you recall,' she tells him.

Gus is picturing his father, a competition angler, casting his line from a sea wall. 'We need some beer,' he says.

Rowena's face falls. There is a glass jug of water on the table, with a nasturtium flower floating among the ice cubes.

'No problem.'

They hear Gus running up the stairs, singing, 'Ah, yes, I rhemember it whell.' He comes back with a six-pack. 'Mr Fix-it,' thinks Rowena.

'There you go.' He puts a can at each place, three at his own. 'Cheers!' He rips one open and raises it in a toast to Rowena, as if he hadn't given her the cold shoulder that morning. The others pour their beer into glasses.

'To Rowena. And the Nautilus!' says Celeste.

'And all who sail in her,' adds Gus.

'Superb. Where did you learn to cook like this?' asks Francis. 'If it's not an impertinent question. I mean – where are your people from?'

Her people? A group of shadowy, benign figures, waiting to welcome her.

It is impertinence. She wouldn't have dreamed of asking Celeste that question, but her own colouring had always given even strangers the right to ask where she comes from. Even drunken backpackers on the tube. She replies in an exhausted voice, 'I come from a long line of orphans. My father was Scottish. He was killed on the Burma Front.'

'So you're half Burmese?' Francis looks pleased, as if he's been proved right.

Rowena worries that in declaring her father first she has betrayed her mother. And why does she always have to mention the Burma Front? It's as if she were saying defensively, 'I'm as British as you are.'

'My mother was Indian. I was brought up in Scotland by my aunt, until she died. Then I was sent to an English boarding school.'

'Ah, educated in England, were you?'

'No, I was educated in Scotland, and then I went to school in England.'

In fact, since leaving Scotland, Rowena has continued her education by reading novels, learning from fictional characters' mistakes and faux pas. Thus she was taught to hold a wine glass by its stem, always to wear stockings in town, to cut flowers under running water, never to smoke in the street or apply make-up in restaurants, nor to eat the rinds of soft cheeses, in public anyway. At Chestnuts, she had sucked the stringy rind of mousetrap cheese so sharp it almost cut your mouth. And at Chestnuts she had discovered a book called *Enemies of Promise* in a box of jumble donated by a local philanthropist: 'There is no more sombre enemy of good art than the pram in the hall.' Not long afterwards, a twin pram took up residence in the school entrance hall, for the Waddiloves produced, belatedly, a pair of cherubs in porcelain and gold, with eyes as blue as sapphires and cupid's-bow mouths, putti in buster suits, Castor and Pollux in nappies; and Rowena's academic career came to an end. Soon there were no pupils, no staff, just Rowena and the Waddilove family.

Celeste, noticing Rowena fold her arms to stop herself scratching, asks Gus if he has had a good day.

'Dead,' he answers, shattering a poppadom. 'You?'

'Oh, mixed. I met rather a peculiar woman. Gus, I wonder, if one of those silver scooters comes your way, I might have first refusal? That woman had one, and then I saw two more from the bus window.'

'Micro-scooter? For one of the great-grandchildren? They've all got to have one, kids, haven't they?' He hesitates, frowning. 'Sure. I'll see what I can do. Mind you, I'll be overrun with people trying to offload them when the craze is over, if you're prepared to wait.'

'I need it now. An adult model.'

Gus, head on one side, sizes her up and decides that a child's scooter will do her.

'Tell you what though, Celeste, you'd have to promise me you'd use it for lawful purposes only. I heard some old dear in South Norwood had her bag snatched by a couple of muggers on scooters. What would you call them, scuggers?'

'I promise not to go scugging in South Norwood,' says Celeste, delighted that Gus sees her as perpetrator rather than old dear or victim. She catches fragments of Francis's monologue to Rowena: '. . . Artists' Rifles' and '. . . decorated'.

And Rowena's preoccupied comment, 'I suppose they would have been.'

Gus's reference to great-grandchildren has given her a presentiment of exclusion. She can see Celeste doting while shrill-voiced scootering brats turn her polished floors into a dirt track, intellectual kids with thin necks and curly hair and high foreheads using the Nautilus as a velodrome. Out of the blue, she wonders what happened to all Aunt Mysie's belongings. Her furniture. Her books, her records, her clothes. Where the hell were Aunt Mysie's things? What vultures had taken them? Were some of them mouldering in the attic at Chestnuts, or had they been plundered for dressing-up, for charades at Killdeer Castle? The shot-silk evening dress, the evening purse of liquid cut steel. Rowena can remember clearly a labelled trunk, a black mortarboard, or trenchard as Aunt Mysie had called it, with its yellow tassel. She feels the silky strands, tangled and coming loose in her fingers. It had been their plan that she should follow in Aunt Mysie's footsteps to St Andrews, the rocky promontory where Mysie had worn the yellow beak of the Bejantine. The old tide of shame that she had not had the grit to pursue her aunt's dream washes over her. She is as dishonoured as if she'd been sent down.

'Peculiar in what way, that woman you met, apart from the scooter?' asks Francis.

'Oh, full of good intentions, but there was something rather forsaken about her.'

'So she was on the side of the angels?'

'I'm not sure. Claimed to know an artist but plainly had no visual sense whatsoever.'

Rowena is struck by fear that the others regard her as a forsaken soul who has weaseled her way into their circle, one step up from a bag lady who, out of their charity, they have allowed to serve them. What a fool she's been. The writing on the wall has been there all the time, the writing in the hall, on envelopes and postcards addressed to Celeste, in the ringing of her telephone. It's possible that Celeste's family has even been in the Nautilus while she has been working elsewhere in the building. She blocks out the accusing voice of Bernadette of the Caring Options Agency.

'Somebody threw an egg at me the other night,' she hears herself saying into the silence that has fallen.

Gus hears again the snap of a twig in the bushes as he was loading the van, but this time he feels a rustle of unease. What kids? Whose?

Celeste puts down her fork, as if she's seen something disgusting on her plate.

'Extraordinary,' said Francis. 'Only last week I was standing at a bus stop, it was a glorious morning, I was looking forward to meeting a friend for lunch, reading the *LRB*, keeping an eye out for the bus. When, suddenly, I was blinded! Deluged in milk! In a shocking white-out that left me gasping. My spectacles, hair, clothes, the pristine *LRB*, all spattered, drenched. Some schoolgirls had thrown a carton of milk under the wheels of a passing car, and it exploded. It was hard not to take it personally, as I was the only person in the line of fire, but I tried not to show any reaction, merely stepped back from the kerb where two or three other people were waiting, all staring into space as if nothing had happened.

'Was it me, something about my face, my clothes, my absorption in print, an unconscious air of contentment or superiority that antagonised them? Had they gone into the shop with the express intent of purchasing the milk to exact revenge on me?'

'Was it the Express Dairy?' says Gus.

'Did they simply hate me for being old? I set out spruce and purposeful, and I slunk home humiliated, a smelly pensioner who had outlived his right to stand on the pavement, tail between my legs like a mangy fox snouting through a bin bag. You know that cringing way they have of running, bundling up their legs.'

Gus sees the scrubby grass in front of a block of flats, overflowing dustbins, nappy sacks scattered. He can smell the sickly-sweet pink scent of them.

'And no doubt those girls forgot me the moment they were on the bus. It was just a cheap laugh to them. I was filled with the most violent fantasies of revenge, quite disproportionate to their crime. I would be ashamed to tell you what went through my head. But you know, Rowena, I got over it, I got over it. As you will. You may even remember a time in your own youth when you would have found it amusing. The trick is to create your own mental climate when you're out and about, do a crossword or look at the trees and imagine yourself back in time, in the great North Wood as all this was once, then you can transcend the nastiness around you.'

'But you –' Rowena begins to point out, then says, 'I have got over it. I don't know why I mentioned it.'

'Spooky,' Gus remarks. 'First milk, then an egg. It's

almost as if somebody, or some*thing*, out there is trying to make pancakes of us Nautilans. All it needs now is for somebody to throw flour over Celeste or me.' He takes out his mobile. 'Get me the Pancake Police. I want to report two serious incidents of assault and battery.'

Celeste just smiles, shaking her head, her earrings catching the light. Rowena claps her hands to her head. Naked lobes. Not even a pair of workaday silver rings. How hideous. Worse, unbelievably, the thin gold chain that always skims her collarbones isn't there. She watches it slithering link by link, slowly at first then accelerating beyond hope, down the vortex of the glass bath. Giving the lie to one of her most valued tenets: you will seldom regret washing your hair but you will almost always regret not having washed it.

'Don't look so stricken,' Francis is saying. 'It was only milk after all. Might have been acid. Of course, my day was ruined, and I had to pay for my suit to be cleaned. Damned stuff even got into my shoes and my bus-pass wallet. Had to apply for a new one. Which meant queuing for hours in the post office. First time I went, it was closed, thanks to a ram raid with a JCB, so I had another wasted trip.'

'If you steal my purse, you steal my money. If you steal my time, you steal my life,' says Rowena flatly. 'Excuse me.'

She folds her napkin and runs upstairs, even if everybody will think her own cooking has made her dash to the bathroom.

'Wonder if I should risk it?' Gus helps himself to more. 'Oh well, they used to call me Iron Guts in t'army. Laurence Harvey, *Room at the Top*,' he explains, blobbing cucumber raita on to the pile, patently never officer material himself.

Francis has been disingenuous. Much of his pleasure on that bright morning came from a review trouncing the latest book by an old acquaintance, and the anticipation of sharing it over lunch in Elena's *L'Étoile*.

'How different life is from art,' he says. 'I might have admired those girls, with never a thought for the havoc they caused, if they had been maenads in a painting, garlanded with flowers, leading a white bull off to some pastoral rout. Functional illiterates, no doubt, avenging themselves on the world of words. It's frequently puzzled me, you know, that there's so often a tin of white paint spilled at bus stops, splashed all over the pavement. Perhaps I've found the answer to that particular mystery.'

Gus rolls his eyes at Celeste.

'No use crying over spilt milk,' he says. 'Or paint. Have you given Natterjack a call yet, Celeste?'

'I'll do it in the morning. I wonder if I should go and see if Rowena's all right?'

'I'll go,' says Gus, leaving the table.

'Laurence Harvey,' muses Celeste. 'What a beautiful man. A Litvak, of course. I suppose Gus has a slight look of him, in a coarser way. I adored him in *The Manchurian Candidate*.'

'"Care to pass the time with a little solitaire?"' asks Francis. 'I wonder what that fellow's up to? Doesn't seem appropriate, going to a lady's room like that. In the circumstances.'

Francis reaches over to Gus's place for another beer and offers it to Celeste, who declines. He opens it, saying, 'To tell you the truth, Celeste, I'm sick to death of all the filth and noise and aggression, of being caught up in other people's violence. The constant sirens and yellow witness boards everywhere. The systematic destruction of our way of life. Perhaps it's time for our generation to fight back, form bands of vigilantes, take to the streets and execute summary justice. The *alter kockers*' revenge.'

'Don't be ridiculous, Francis. Maybe it's time the Nautilus threw a party. We've become too insular, not part of the local community any more. Remember the summer picnics, how everybody used to come? You know, a while ago I was approached about a scheme to open interesting buildings to the public for a day. I turned it down but now, with Rowena here . . . perhaps it would be possible to participate after all.'

'No! That's a terrible idea, Celeste.'

He sandwiches her hand, grinding her rings into her fingers, between his. 'You and I, my dear, have had our fifteen minutes of fame. To try to grab another would be undignified. And would you really want *hoi polloi* traipsing around dropping litter and looking for the toilets, or ignoramuses from some so-called heritage or style magazine portraying our poor old Nautilus as a superannuated folly, or you as Gloria Swanson in *Sunset Boulevard*? I'm thinking of Rowena too – she's got quite enough on her plate as it is. If she thinks she's being exploited, she'll be off like a startled deer.'

Celeste wrenches her hand away. *Alter kockers*; he'd got it from her in the first place. Folly. Fifteen minutes of fame. She watches him wipe a folded piece of nan bread round his plate and put it in the mouth that had uttered these blasphemies. Rowena's abandoned plate, in contrast to the abstract expressionism of Gus's smeared colours and flavours, is a neat palette of separate cones and swirls.

'Immortal Piety, how oft I sobbing sought thee,' whispers a voice in Francis's head. So what? He was ten years old when he had started that poem. OK, thirteen. All poets lie about their age when confronted with their juvenilia. Betjeman had even admitted to it. 'Desire illimitable . . .' there, on the second line, inspiration had dried.

'I can't think that Rowena feels exploited. She positively takes tasks upon herself, quite beyond the call of duty. Like this meal. And I've suggested a cleaner to help out but she refuses. I've heard her singing as she goes about her work.'

'Talks to herself too. What is this local community to which you referred, anyway? Perhaps there *isn't* any such thing as society any more. That was a self-fulfilling prophecy if there ever was one. Tell me, where are the Brownies and Guides of yesteryear, the elfin Wolf Cubs panting to polish your car or take your manuscript to the post for a bob?'

Where indeed is the manuscript that waits in vain for the second coming of Bob-A-Job Week?

Oh, do shut up, you tedious old goat, bleating out your sententious jeremiad. No wonder passers-by feel obliged to douse you in milk.

'Vulpine, the Wolf Cubs. The Brownies were, again by definition, elfin. And still are. The Nautilus is merely in need of a few running repairs, which I have in hand. As you well know, it was designed as a working community at the heart of the wider community, and it shall be again, so I'll thank you not to write either of us off just yet. And if I'm

Gloria Swanson, that makes you a mummified monkey.'

It strikes her as absurd that she and Francis are squabbling again like an old married couple. He is sitting in Arkady's place, so smug in his pink pullover. Strange endgame. Ultimately, she will have spent more time with Francis than with her own dear love, the father of her children, the missing grandfather and great-grandfather robbed of the tranquil last movement of his life's concerto.

All this nonsense about taking to the streets. If Francis were to study the *South London Press*, he would see daily evidence of the perpetual struggle of good and evil; the voluntary workers, gardeners, dancers and athletes, the local heroes versus the gunmen, knifers, arsonists and thieves. As for his sentimental maundering about children in uniform – he'd always made himself scarce when the Woodcraft Folk held their annual bazaar in the Nautilus grounds. And he'd positively loathed that one-time resident, what was his name, who became an adherent of the Kindred of the Kibbo Kift, donning the green cowl and tunic of John Hargrave's breakaway movement from Baden-Powell's Scouts, and arming himself with a crossbow. Black Stag, that was what he called himself. Hargrave was White Fox.

Although Celeste sympathised with some of the Kift's social ideas, and applauded the marching of their greenshirts in opposition to Mosley's blackshirts, she had not joined. The only uniform she had worn since her schooldays was that of a nursing auxiliary for a while during the war. Black Stag recruited vigorously for the cause and several of the Nautilans metamorphosed, briefly, into animals and birds, and Frau Stumpfenhose was wounded by an arrow, caught in crossbow fire. Celeste remembers Black Stag's efforts to persuade Arkady that his aquiline face and bright eyes made him a natural Bold Eagle. Francis, too, had resisted, declining the suggestion that he call himself Pale Weasel.

Rowena, hunched on the edge of her bed, hears the rap of her shell and stiffens, every nerve silently screaming, Go away! Everything always broken and lost. Leave me alone! Tap tap tap. The door opens, how dare it, there stands Gus.

Gus sees her sitting there with her arms crossed in a W, hands gripping her shoulders, as if she will start rocking. Don't go all Cadbury's on me, girl, I can't handle it. 'They are all Cadbury's,' his aunt who had a kiosk on the front at Westcliff used to say of her customers, the flakes and fruit-and-nut cases.

'Anything I can do?'

Rowena realises she must look deranged. Her fingers press painfully into her bones. She is making a show of herself. She has ruined the evening. She must speak, salvage what she can.

'Rowena? You OK? Are you feeling ill?'

'Sorry. I just realised I'd lost something. My gold chain.'

She feels an easing of tension as she speaks, even though her voice is thick with unshed tears.

'When did you last have it?'

'I don't know. I never take it off.' She unclasps her arms, saying, 'It's not important.'

'Has it got sentimental value? Only I could get one for you. What kind was it?'

'A Belcher,' she has to admit. 'It's nothing special. I just like it.'

'I suppose you've looked in the shower? Silly question. Have you checked your towel?'

'My towel?'

'Go on, it's worth a try.'

He lounges in the bathroom doorway, breathing the atmosphere of dissolved lavender.

'You're a genius!'

She holds out a blue towel, with a gold chain dangling from a pulled loop of thread.

'It's what I do. Find things. Allow me.' He clasps it over her bowed neck.

'Thank you. Gus –?'

'That's my name.'

'It doesn't matter. Nothing.'

'Go on, spit it out.'

'Well – this morning, you walked right past me. I wondered if I'd done anything . . .'

'You thought I was blanking you? I didn't think you saw me, I didn't want to startle you into falling off your perch.'

'Oh.' She runs the chain through her fingers. 'We'd better go down. They'll be wondering what we're doing.'

The possibility of not going downstairs flashes between them. Rowena reaches for her gold earrings.

'Hello, Sailor.' Gus picks up a blue velvet sailor doll from the window sill and scrutinises the worn pile of its body and the dented, eggshell-crazed face, the scarlet traces of its painted smile. He examines the label on its foot, but the maker's name has long since worn away.

Rowena almost snatches the doll.

'You know Oscar Wilde's definition of a cynic.'

Gus holds up his hands and backs away. 'Hey. Take it easy. I didn't say a word.'

So he has discovered her Achilles heel.

On the stairs he says, over his shoulder, 'So tell me about the egg.'

'It was nothing. I was just walking home after spending the day with friends, and some boys in a car threw an egg at me.'

'Couldn't your friends have driven you, or got you a cab?'

'Well, they offered of course, but it was such a lovely night I preferred to walk.'

Gus's silence indicates that he doesn't think much of her friends, and suggests that they don't think much of her. Rowena is furious with him. Now she is not only a person who gets pelted with eggs in the street but she has so-called friends who are happy to let her risk being attacked. She relives her parting from the Dunlops.

Sylvia: George will drive you home, won't you, darling?

George, changed out of his suit into shorts, lounging in a garden chair: I wish you'd said. I wouldn't have put the car away.

Rowena, twisting the carrier-bag handle round her fingers: No, really. It isn't far. And I do honestly feel like a walk.

George, his inner thighs spread on the seat, calves like rugby balls and feet in flip-flops: Well, if you insist.

Sylvia: Take care then, love.

As Rowena remembers, a library book flashes into her vision, *The Lonely Passion of Judith Hearne*. Yes, in the Dunlops' eyes she is spinster Judith Hearne, barely tolerated, secretly mocked and ultimately unloved. Gus is saying, 'Francis and the milk, though. You have to laugh. Funnily enough, there did used to be an Express Dairy on that corner. Anyhow, let us know if you ever want a lift to Sainsbury's.'

You could cut the atmosphere with a knife, he thinks, as they come back to the dining room.

'It's so nice to be using the Norwood dinner service again,' says Celeste to Rowena, picking up a side plate. 'It was made by Greta Wenzel. Autumn leaves on a wet pavement. It was shown at the Festival of Britain. The Nautilus had its own pavilion, and the Queen came in to look at some of our designs. Are you feeling better?'

'We were getting worried.' Francis's tone is acid. 'I was about to mount a rescue mission armed with a bottle of Pepto-Bismol.'

He notes Rowena's discomfiture with satisfaction. A result, as they say. He is unaware that while cleaning his chamber, Rowena found his patent remedy solidified and separated into two shades of pink, which reminded her of a packet honeycomb mould pudding she sometimes made at Chestnuts for a Sunday treat. The expiry date had passed three years previously, and Rowena dropped the bottle into a bin liner.

'Immeasurably better,' Rowena tells Celeste. 'Thanks to Gus.'

She sees that some further explanation is needed. 'I suddenly realised my gold chain was missing and he found it for me.'

'And you've put on some pretty earrings,' says Francis.

5

'Natterjack. Jacki speaking. How may I *help* you?'

The timbre of the young woman's voice, suggesting shade cards of unsuitable colours, almost makes Celeste replace the receiver without speaking. Better perhaps to let paint flake off, mould run riot, blisters of damp proliferate, and leave it for someone else to deal with after she's gone. But she can no more betray the Nautilus than a mother could abandon an ailing child, and to let it go to rack and ruin would be to betray Arkady as well. Besides, some of the family, who threatened periodically to get workmen in on her behalf, might themselves decide to move in one day.

'It's a specialist job. A very unusual building.'

'No problem. We specialise in the artistic and architecturally challenged. We're working on a church conversion at the minute, as it happens. Sorry, did you give me your name at all? Right. Would that be Miss or Mrs Silverstone?'

'Princess, or Professor will do, and it's Zylberstein,' Celeste snaps, and then spells it out for her, adding that Mrs will suffice.

'Bear with me a moment, you can never find a pen when you need one, can you? Hullo-o? Are you still with me? Can you just run that name past me again? I've got Zebra, Yoghurt, Lemur, Bravo . . .'

They agree that Natterjack will come round that evening to assess the work with no obligation.

'I was given your name by Mr Crabb,' says Celeste, wondering as she speaks whose side Gus will be on.

'Oh yes, Gus. He's put quite a lot of work our way, and we've been able to reciprocate with various bits and bobs we've picked up.'

Bits and bobs – a few saints' bones, gargoyles, pieces of plate, a rood screen or two? Vandalising, stripping. Celeste thinks of the two stone lions which were stolen from the gates of the Home and Hospital for Incurables recently. It seems there is no theft so low that somebody will not stoop to it, or wall too high for greed to scale. Once upon a time the Nautilus workshops could have presented the hospital with a pair of replacement lions.

'I'll look forward to seeing you this evening then, Miss, er, Natterjack.'

Celeste puts down the phone and stands with her arms at her sides in the motionless air between the end of the conversation and her next action, and suddenly, she's petrified, her feet encased in a stone plinth. Outside, a magpie's strident cries rebound from perch to perch. 'I feel distinctly odd,' she says aloud.

After a while she goes into her kitchen to make coffee. She picks up a glass egg timer half filled with stripes of coloured sand and turns it over in her hand watching the grains trickling through. *A Present From Alum Bay*, from her daughter Susannah on a trip to the Isle of Wight; a little girl on a summer day long ago. Time reverses and Susannah stands on the beach in her red knitted bathing suit; Celeste can see clearly her smile, her topaz-coloured eyes beneath the fringe of dark bobbed hair with sunstruck copper glints, the powdered sand on the long legs. Her arms open to embrace, to clasp the child's body to her own; how could she ever have let go, allowed that day to end? The green translucent sea flounced with white, white wings of gulls and sails against blue sky, samphire in flower on the cliffs behind them, the tin spade and bucket painted with jolly crabs and starfish; it is all there in the egg timer's glass, but the sand sifts, the crystalline sharpness of the picture blurs, as the smell of coffee pervades and the pot which has been hiccuping intermittently gives its concluding spurt.

Suddenly dizzy, she sits down. In the doorway looms a tall stooped figure in a black hooded, girdled robe, leaning on a scythe, grasping an hourglass in a skeletal hand. His hood falls back to reveal a grinning death's head. Celeste wards him off, holding out the egg timer like a talisman. His robe turns white, his bones assume flesh, his features change into a face of ancient wisdom as the Grim Reaper softens into Father Time, and fades and vanishes. A kindlier personification, but still immutable, still in thrall to the trickling sand.

During the conversation with the Natterjack girl, Celeste had been aware of tremors of anxiety unconnected with the matter in hand. Now, shaken by the apparition, she wonders if she could have had a mild heart attack. She sips a cup of coffee, and decides that she is absolutely fine, but her heart has been attacked by the need to hold a baby in her arms. She feels a baby's open-mouthed kiss on her face.

But suppose, she wonders, each grain of sand represents a moment of happiness? Should I not then be overcome with gratitude? *Au bas* the old fool with his sickle and egg timer; are we eggs to be boiled to some phantom's taste? I'll decide when I'm done and ready for the eggcup. Meanwhile, I can turn and turn the glass and hold memory and time in my hand.

She returns to the bedroom and slides out one of the integral drawers under her bed. It is packed with files of photographs. There is the album she never opens. Nevertheless, faces trapped in sepia are imprinted on her memory; twin boys looking out with dark eyes under peaked caps which look too big, caps which would fit the men they will never become; children whose mouths look hurt before anything terrible has happened.

She studies a group portrait of her great-grandchildren. Dark and fair, solemn, cross, posing or mucking about for the camera, skins ranging from olive to porcelain, they look out at her, making her smile back at them. The vivid stripes and colours of their clothes are worlds away from the heavy cloth and starched frocks of the locked album, but this one, little Violet who insisted on wearing her fairy dress for the photograph, she has the same eyes, the hurt mouth, the skinny legs of the sepia children, her great-aunts and uncles, or distant cousins, once removed.

Celeste places the photograph on her bedside table. Human beings are not birds who drive their young from the nest to fend for themselves. What is the point of creating, and then living apart from the people you love the best? Intellectually, she understands her children's decision to move away; that would be fine if this life was just a segment of time in which we go our ways secure in the knowledge of spending eternity together. But now there were all these grandchildren and all these empty rooms. Would any of them really ever claim their inheritance? Alone in her chamber, she is ashamed to remember that the Nautilus was conceived as an earthly paradise. Who is happy here? A water pipe judders somewhere in the building as a tap is turned on. Bad vibes. The conversation with Francis comes back to her, and at once the Natterjack project seems doomed to failure.

Fingering a necklace of wild pearls, from Freshwater Bay, smaller than a baby's first teeth, she wonders how artistic could somebody with that quasi-corporate-speak be? The girl sounded like an escapee from one of those call stations, vast as aircraft hangars, where prisoners are shackled to their headphones until they have sold their quota of double glazing, and also her grasp of the phonetic alphabet did not inspire confidence.

Into what were Natterjack converting that church? A wine bar? Deconsecrated luxury apartments? Sorry, God, you've fallen behind with the payments and we're repossessing your house. She thinks of the synagogue in Brixton, abandoned for years, wreathed in ivy, beautiful, potent and secret in its neglect. Regenerated as the Eurolink Business Centre. She had been pleased when the green letters of its new name began to fall off, perhaps thrown down in anger by the building itself. But they had been replaced and now who would know there had ever been a synagogue in Brixton? Or a Jewish orphanage in Norwood.

Instead of brooding, Celeste decides she will get out more to visit the family, instead of waiting like an *alterkocker* for them to visit her. She still has her driving licence. She will go to the garage right now and check her car. No doubt it needs a service, but then there will be no stopping her.

Francis is in the hall. The post has come. Francis is in a fury, shaking a fistful of letters at her.

'What fresh hell is this? Now I've got to go all the way to the Palace to collect some damned thing I don't want!'

'What, the Queen's medal for poetry, at last?'

He stomps past her. 'What's the point of employing a housekeeper if she's always got her nose in a book or is scribbling her wretched poetry instead of answering the door to the postman? Useless article!'

Celeste retrieves her own post and takes it outside. It is hardly Rowena's fault that the post arrives at all hours. Francis is so inconsistent; yesterday he was accusing Celeste of exploitation. She sees that the garden is on the verge of becoming a wilderness, with seedheads spitting white feathers everywhere, pieces of sculpture and ventifacts lost in the grass. She'd no idea that Rowena wrote poetry, and is annoyed by her own lack of perception.

Gus, driving along with a porcelain phrenology head in the passenger seat, winking at a woman waiting on the traffic island, avoids thinking about the photograph he glimpsed while fishing for a lighter in the glove compartment. It is the picture of his children that used to dangle from the mirror, of his six-year-old son, Gus Jr, also known as Little Gus, as he himself once was, and his five-year-old daughter Kizzy, short for Kezia. His wife Carole chose the name, saying it was only fair as she had no choice in the naming of her firstborn, even though she had added Zephyr as his middle name, poor kid. Kizzy was called after the little girl in the TV adaptation of Rumer Godden's *The Diddakoi*. If Gus had a pound for every time he'd heard Carole say, 'I always remember the bit where Joe the horse that used to pull the wagon dies, and he's lying in the meadow and the Admiral tells Kizzy, "This is just his old clothes, Kiz. He doesn't need them any more."' She'd come out with it when her dad died, and at the demise of several goldfish and hamsters, always in floods. He doesn't want to be thinking about these family things. His mother and sister aren't speaking to him. Even Dad, who was always on his side, had said, 'I'm disappointed in you, son.'

A scene from his schooldays presents itself. The classroom door crashes open, Big Gus strides up to Mr Jordan's desk and grabs a fistful of red braces and candy-striped shirt, his massive knuckles bunching under the smaller man's chin forcing his mouth open into a buck-toothed gape beneath his grey moustache. As Big Gus hoists him out of his chair, the teacher's shirt rips, exposing a vest tucked into the waistband of pink paisley boxer shorts.

'Nobody calls my boy a liar. Putting my boy in detention for something he never done.'

Afterwards, boys used to call out behind Mr Jordan's back, 'What colour are they today, sir?'

Only, as everybody but Big Gus knew, Little Gus *had* cheated in the history exam.

Big Gus was an electrician, now retired, and it was while accompanying his dad, toting his miniature box of tools, that Gus developed a curiosity about antiques, and other people's houses. One house in particular:

Whiteladies, where his father had undertaken a complete rewiring, a long job which entailed unscrewing innumerable fluted brass light switches and fittings and replacing frayed brown twisted flexes with clean white plastic cables. Whiteladies comes to mind now as he drives along with his silent porcelain companion.

White-painted gates opened on to a drive bordered by white flowers and silver-leaved bushes. Dad introduced Little Gus as his apprentice to two white-haired old ladies in pale dresses. A white cockatoo with a sulphur-yellow crest shrieked as the housekeeper led Dad and Little Gus to a ballroom with a shrouded piano and glass doors opening on to a flight of steps that fanned down to a sunken garden with the sound of the sea and bees in the white lavender. The skeletons of two chandeliers stood on the ballroom floor with all their prismatic lustres, and tendrils, leaves, fruits and trumpet-shaped flowers of bluish milkglass arranged in circles round them. A tall girl was dipping the pieces, each suspended from a fragile wire hook, into an enormous bowl of soapsuds and rinsing them in clean water.

'You can make yourself useful,' said the housekeeper, handing Gus a glass cloth.

Later, she plonked down a tray of lemonade and caraway-seed cake saying, 'I've got my beady eye on you. Just in case you was thinking of slipping a lustre or two into your pocket. Every piece is numbered and accounted for.'

Much of that day has faded but whenever he takes the kids to the rookery off Streatham Common, the white garden there triggers a memory of faceted glass and soap bubbles flashing lights, and a girl saying, 'There must be a million, trillion, zillion rainbows in this room.'

He'd managed to put back the prism he'd secreted in the ruler pocket of his dungarees, without anybody seeing. He'd wanted it so much; he'd *needed* it. Perhaps he has been trying to get back to Whiteladies all his life, perhaps he had seen something of it in the Nautilus. Could Rowena have been that girl, was that where he remembered her from? Maybe he was forgetting something crucial. The girl had on a big white apron, but was she a servant or a daughter of the house, an heiress, even Estella to his Pip? Maybe he'd missed out on a fortune along the way. She should have used vinegar on those lustres.

As he calls Big Gus on his mobile he catches the smirk of a woman in a minicab, identifying archetypal White Van Man.

'Pops, how's it going?'

He realises he has used the children's name for their grandpa, and also that Carole has probably been on the phone, or worse, blackening his name.

'Gus? I was just thinking about you. Carole and the kids were down at the weekend. When are you going to see sense –'

'Sorry, Dad, you're breaking up.'

He holds the phone away from his ear, then says, 'Dad, you remember that house, where we did the chandeliers?'

'Whiteladies. Why?' Dad's hoarse voice sounds suspicious.

'Whiteladies, yes. Can you recall a young girl there, she'd have been quite bit older than me, dark? A coloured girl?'

'I don't recall there being any coloured people round here in them days. It's a country club now. Whiteladies

Manor. They have a lot of conferences there, corporate entertaining. They've put in a mini golf course –'

'Never mind. Forget it. Got to go. Take care, Dad. Love to Mum.'

He breaks the connection, dismissing a corporate Whiteladies from his mind and thinking that there was probably some hospital appointment or something he should have asked about, then swerves violently as a woman thrusts a buggy into the road from between two parked cars. Some people shouldn't be allowed to have kids. Sweating, he takes the next left and finds himself heading for the flat where Carole and the children are living. He has a key, nicked from Gus Jr. Unless Carole has had the locks changed. He can't see her doing that because anything which involves ringing up a tradesman throws her into a panic. He always has to do it for her. Carole says that the children get upset after seeing him, so he has reluctantly agreed to stay away for a while. He had to, Carole holds all the aces.

Gus drives into the Belfairs Estate and parks outside Mitchell House, built by the LCC in a spirit of post-war optimism. Hot air blasts up from the asphalt, and the smell of cut grass comes from the lawn with the notice saying 'No Ball Games' where one pigeon struts, cooing, in pursuit of another and a dog forages in a bag of rubbish. He can hear birdsong and the bell-like call of a caged bird. There is not a soul about although music thuds from a parked car. The gate of the adventure playground is locked. He looks up at the balconies cluttered with junk and washing and sees an old man, so gaunt that it looks as though he's left the hanger in his shirt, leaning on the rail as if staring out to sea and wondering how the hell he landed up here.

Gus takes the concrete stairs to the second floor, goes along the walkway and rings the bell of number 34. As he expects, there is no answer. He puts his key to the keyhole. Carole has had the locks changed.

'I didn't think she had it in her,' he tells Rita in the Gipsy Rose Café. 'Yeah, yeah, I know.'

'I didn't say a word.'

'You didn't have to, I could see what you were thinking.'

He finishes his drink with a melancholy gurgle of Diet Coke siphoned between rocks of ice. The childish sound is an echo of his kids. Belfairs Estate, the exotic bird calling to the free birds from its cage, the old man on the balcony. He could hear the silence inside the flat when he lifted the flap of the letter box, sense unmade bunk beds, scattered toys and clothes and breakfast dishes in the sink.

'You didn't need to put a straw in this, Reet, I can just about manage a glass, and I could have done without the umbrella and salad. You're running a caff, not the Ritz.'

'Somebody got out of bed on the wrong side. It's one of my Summer Sparklers. Shame it's clouded over, it was beautiful earlier.'

Rita removes the ashtray where Gus has dumped his paper parasol and a drowned sprig of mint; as the mother of a teenage daughter she is hardened to criticism. There are days when she slaps down customers' orders in front of them with the tacit threat that if they don't finish it, either they'll sit there till they do or it will be served up cold next time they come in.

Her daughter, Rhiannon, might have stepped from an illustration in a book of Celtic fairy tales; one could imagine her, straight-backed, green-kirtled, side-saddle on a caparisoned palfrey passing a stylised thicket of medieval roses; her proud demeanour suggests a princess in captivity, destined to grace the Round Table but bound by some enchantment to wipe down the oilcloths of the Gipsy Rose Café. Rita lives in fear that Rhiannon's hobbity father will materialise to claim her.

'So what's your friend having?' says Rita, jerking her thumb at the phrenology head sitting on the table with all its characteristics mapped out in black. 'Hasn't got much to say for himself, has he? Uh-oh, here comes Trouble.'

Rhiannon, disguised as a schoolgirl, comes in, slams down a tapestry bag of books, slides on to the red banquette opposite Gus, scatters raindrops from her hair and picks up the head.

'Can I have him? He would be perfect for my art project.'

'It's for a customer. Anyway, who's to say it's a he?'

'For my gender studies then. Go on, Gus. I really need it.'

'Gender studies my backside,' snorts stocky Rita.

'Mother, must you be so vulgar? I'll pay you for it, Gus. I'm getting a Saturday job soon. Mum will give me an advance.'

'In your dreams.'

'You so don't want me to pass my exams, do you?'

'Saturday job? Was that a flying pig just passed the window? It's as much as you can do to help out in here occasionally. I am not wasting good money on that bald bonce and that's final. If you ask me he looks mental. You only want it to add to all the other junk in your bedroom, admit it. And I blame you, Gus, for the state of madam's room.'

6

Rowena had been halfway down the stairs when she heard Francis's voice in the hall. Sick with disbelief at the words 'Useless article', she'd shrunk back to her chamber. Distractedly, she slid back her cupboard door and saw a lurking blue plastic carrier bag. She plunged in her hand and pulled out, not the manuscript that Francis dreads, but a sheaf of junk mail from pizza joints, estate agents, minicab firms, health clubs, lonely hearts agencies; she had stuffed it into the bag, meaning to bin it on her exit from 15a Formosa Road, where she was the only tenant who ever swept the hall. She'd left no forwarding address, but she'd brought this rubbish, including dead leaves and dirty tissues, from her old life into the Nautilus. What am I, a litter bin? She fell back on the bed and stared at a stain on the ceiling, a cloud that had tracked her down and found her here. Pipe-Cleaner Man, her last client with Caring Options, returned to haunt her, and he brought fear of expulsion and disgrace. Rowena had been his home help, visiting twice daily, getting his breakfast and settling him down for the night. His name was actually Mr Apsley but, with his dense fuzz of grey-white hair and skinny limbs protruding from his pyjamas, he resembled a figure made from twisted pipe-cleaners, the father of the family which lived in the Chestnuts doll's house.

Clifford's pipe-cleaners, bundles of fleecy sticks with cores of silver wire, and the coloured spills with which he lit his pipe, provided the model-making materials in the art room there, along with cereal packets and the insides of toilet rolls. Giving Mr Apsley a secret nickname was Rowena's defence against his querulous demands and what at times seemed spiteful accidents, with bowls of tomato soup in bed, for example, or boiling his kettle to a blackened hulk. Later she realised that these were merely ploys to make her stay longer, and in time the compassion she felt for him grew almost into affection. It was his layabout son Derek she couldn't stand, a middle-aged slug who from time to time crawled into the spare bed, where she found him curled up in the morning, and who expected her to clear up after him.

It had all ended in tears, Rowena's and Pipe-Cleaner Man's, and if Celeste and Francis were to hear the lies Derek had told about her, if by some hideous mischance they should encounter Bernadette of Caring Options, she had no doubt that she would be out on her ear. Even if they believed Rowena's side of the story, the seeds of doubt would be sown. Foolishly, trustingly, they had demanded to see no references. All it would take would be for one of Celeste's family, for Francis evidently had none, to start poking his or her nose in, out of concern for what Bernadette termed 'the vulnerable elderly at risk'. She should know all about that, judging from the calibre of some of her employees.

Time passes before she creeps down to the dustbins and thence to the laundry. So this is a pantisocracy – a heap of other people's boxers and socks. You put life aside as if you had a laundrybagful of time and personality, then eventually you dip your hand in and find it empty. You are a useless article.

The laundry houses four washing machines, two of them in working order, and two huge driers, all of brushed steel, a row of ironing boards with spidery metal legs hanging from hooks on the wall, a trouser-press and generations of clothes pegs. An airer, worked by rope pulleys, is suspended from the ceiling in the dry atmosphere where the light sparkles as if a million grains of washing powder are dancing in the shafts of sunshine from the porthole windows. Although she has swept the cobwebs from the floor and ceiling, still from time to time some long-lost garment surfaces, a pair of red silk knickers polka-dotted with mildew, the child's sock so coated in dust that she thought it was a dead mouse when it blocked the nozzle of the vacuum cleaner.

Rowena likes this room. Normally, she has no objection to laundry work and, post-Chestnuts, has always positively enjoyed washing and ironing. Oh, the bliss of London launderettes after years of scrubbing collars and boiling nappies, underpants and handkerchiefs when all the staff had left the school, there was no money for laundry bills and the obsolete twin-tub had died. Before signing on with Caring Options she had spent a happy year at the Sunray Laundry behind Lordship Lane; she had often wished she'd stayed there, particularly after the Pipe-Cleaner Man incident.

It was so satisfying to receive a barrow-full of tablecloths, 36s they were called, and vast banqueting cloths stained with food and wine, and supervise the cleaning process, right through to their pressing on the calendar, the enormous ironing maching that left them snowy white and smooth for packing-up and despatch. And there was the 'milking machine' to which the sheets were clipped – she loved the laundry's green and yellow tiles, the rhythm of people working in harmony and the waves of detergent-scented air and the smell of hot linen. She might have stayed there until she retired had it not been for her stupid overreaction to a comment from one of the younger girls. The women were discussing weekend plans and Rowena mentioned that she was looking forward to an open day at Norwood Cemetery, where there would be guided tours and a rare opportunity to go down into the catacombs, where there was an interesting catafalque.

'Get a life, Rowena!' the girl hooted, and she saw that everyone was laughing and she was exposed as somebody who didn't have one. She'd given in her notice.

OK, she thinks as she remembers her embarrassment, whose life should she have got? Sylvia's? Iris should have been Rowena's daughter, anyway. Except that George came with the package. If she hadn't been so picky, she could have had a life with somebody else, that man she'd met in the Horniman museum for example. They'd had tea in the café several times but he'd proved to be a bore.

She crosses her arms over breasts which feel small and soft in her print dress, presses her fingers against her ribs with a jolt of recognition, like that experienced when meeting someone in the street you haven't seen for ages and subconsciously assumed had moved away or died. She hasn't thought about her body for a long time. A tabby cat sidles into her mind, sleek and preternaturally youthful because it has never been allowed to have kittens.

She ought to be a granny by now. The washing machine gargles and voids a sluice of suds into the drains and a wave of hatred for the Dunlops washes over her. They've ruined her street cred with Gus, that of having a life outside the Nautilus. Never again would she select a postcard for them, never telephone again. She'd delete them from her mobile. And what's more, she'd go right now to confront Francis.

Beyond the Purley Way, far beyond the twin towers of Ikea, the woman Celeste encountered at the demo is packing clothes into a plastic sack for charity. Her name is Izzie Ingram. Some of the garments she had devised herself of hopsack, porridgy wool and hodden grey, the habit of an Order which had attracted few adherents and soon disbanded. The founding, and foundering, of her little band of like-minded souls who went about doing good by stealth was just another stage in her pilgrimage through this wicked world and it left her yearning for something indefinable unassuaged. 'We must work!' Who had said that? In work must be her salvation.

She folds a half-finished hair shirt; attaching the combings from the dogs' coats to linen had proved trickier, and stickier, than she'd envisaged. Well, it would keep some poor soul warm, in part; possibly one with something for which to atone.

Izzie feels a dull penitence herself, for one telephone call in particular, and a string of other offences, some not yet committed. The silence of the house, empty of her daughter Miranda, was frazzling her nerves; she'd had to switch off a radio programme about the unwanted girl babies of China. Last night's call to the distinguished artist about whom she had boasted to that woman on the demo had compounded an earlier felony.

'Not interrupting work, am I, Lyris?'

There was a ripping and crumpling noise of paper, the tapping of a paintbrush on a glass jar, as Izzie plunged on.

'I've been feeling guilty. It was so lovely to see you that I'm afraid I outstayed my welcome. I was wondering about that Nautilus place you mentioned. Is it some kind of folly?'

'Not at all. It was a visionary building, housing a working community, much depleted now. They used to have marvellous parties.' A sigh. 'Wot larks, eh?'

'Larks?' Twittering specks, high above the Downs.

Had she ever had larks? At school, larking about in their sky-blue summer dresses?

'Ode to a Skylark', and *Great Expectations*. Joe Gargery was so sad; everything was sad.

At the other end of the line a burst of music, the theme tune of *Emmerdale*, was zapped into a faintly audible murmur of voices. Surely Lyris couldn't prefer some soap opera to talking to a friend? Hooked on a fantasy Yorkshire peopled by homicidal maniacs and serial adulterers, that was sponsored by a washing powder and introduced by two vulgar dogs under the misconception that their washing machine is a television set? Tragic that an artist should be reduced to this. She herself is dogless for the first time she can remember, apart from the ceramic horror of a Dalmatian presented by her husband's mistress on her fiftieth birthday.

'So where exactly is the Nautilus?'

The sound had been turned up again and she had to raise her voice; a fight had apparently broken out in the Woolpack.

Having got the information she needed, Izzie said, 'I musn't keep you from your *work*.'

She felt an electrical charge, the pull of a magnet drawing her to the Nautilus.

She would never ring Lyris again. Let the boot be on the other foot, let Lyris wonder if Izzie is OK, if *her* bad manners have offended. She will send a postcard once she is part of that working community at the Nautilus. But she is aware of a maggoty doubt burrowing through her resolve, and now it emerges. Work. What can she offer? Her experience on the Bench? Hedgehog charity admin? Nurturing skills? Counselling? If all else fails, she is not above getting her hands dirty. She could be a sort of housekeeper. They also serve who only stand and wait.

Izzie has become very familiar with the yellow façade of the Rivoli Ballroom, Brockley Road, as she stands opposite it, hoping for a bus to Crystal Palace. The timetable is obliterated by graffiti. She has got lost several times and a sullen south London rain has begun to fall. Her scooter is folded in her holdall, and now she regrets the sacrifice of her car to the good of the planet. She gazes at the locked Rivoli, picturing formation teams lined up with military precision, the blades of the gentlemen's legs scissoring the ladies' carnation skirts, wheeling, breaking ranks, gliding and bursting into floral extravaganzas in each corner of the room.

Memories of youth club dances whirl past; a wallflower in her mother's toffee-coloured taffeta dress secured to her bra with little gold safety pins, sipping air through a straw from an empty lemonade glass; chairs of splintery bentwood that laddered stockings, the smell of an adolescent boy, soft lips, wisps of blond hair on a spotty chin, the loganberry of shame on her neck in the morning. Her mother snatching away the concealing chiffon scarf to cry, 'It's what one used to expect of the maids! And shop girls. Do you want to end up working in Woolworths?'

School dances. The music goes out of a beautiful waltz when you're dancing boost to boost, Joyce Grenfell used to sing. Not necessarily, if you were clasped in the arms of Sheila O'Rourke, Captain of Nightingale House, who had been your pash since you were in the second form, mooching round the hall to the Sixth Form Skifflers' rendition of 'Love is Strange' with Linda Dobbs, the Lonnie Donegan of the lower sixth, on vocals. Later on, to Mummy's chagrin, Izzie had got a Saturday job in Woolworths. And she'd married Clovis against her advice.

She is joined at the bus stop by a lad scowling out of a hooded sweatshirt, and gradually becomes aware of his resentful aura and shortness of stature as they wait, spurted by passing cars. With his rather large head, he would measure perhaps five feet two on her daughter's old giraffe-shaped height chart. He snuffles a raindrop up his big nose, pushing back his hood; it would not be beyond the skill of a surgeon to make another pair of ears from his, for somebody less generously endowed. A delinquent face, and his jeans inexpertly shortened, so poignantly cobbled by his mother, some care worker or by himself. Poor Titchy, fate has dealt you a bad hand. Sadly, she places him in a Young Offenders' Institution, where he won't stand a chance against the bullies; too small to fight, too mean to play the clown. 'Promise me you'll *try* to stay out of trouble, Titch,' she murmurs. 'Just keep your head down and do your bird.'

'You talking to me?'

Fortunately, the bus arrives and the question seems to demand no answer as he pushes past her. Izzie goes upstairs and finds a seat beside a schoolgirl, who turns round, remarking loudly to her mates, 'Don't you just hate it when somebody plonk they stinky ass down beside you when there's other seats available?'

The words blaze in red graffiti on the air. Titchy turns round, sniggering. Isobel burns. Her scarlet face is a beacon telling all that they were directed at her. She, bathed with cold-pressed olive oil soap, her hair redolent of aloe and rosemary, a faint residue of ecologically sound washing powder in the folds of her skirt? She, arguably the only person on this bus who has ironed her underwear with lavender linen spray? She is damned if she will move to one of the vacant seats she now sees at the front of the bus. If only she had noticed them sooner. She will arrive at the Nautilus tainted by the girl's words, as if she has got something nasty on her shoe. How often she has been wounded by the malice of strangers, and those from whom she would have expected better. On her last visit to the rectory, whence she had scooted to ask permission to put up a poster on the parish noticeboard, inviting applicants to her Order, she had found herself burbling apologies for her absence from church and attempting to explain her own calling.

'Don't get me wrong, Rector. I do believe that there's some Superior Force, some Higher Being, but –'

The rector received her avowal with all the enthusiasm of a vegan who is told that somebody eats hardly any red meat. His eyes glazed over and he could hardly suppress a yawn as she continued, 'I don't think you actually have to go to church to be a Christian or –'

'Yes you do.'

'– or Muslim or whatever, in our multi-faith society.'

'Perhaps you have a point there.' He looked at his watch. 'Well, it's been good talking to you. You'll have to supply your own drawing pins.'

The bus fills with wet black nylon that has absorbed the smell of a thousand fried chickens, and Izzie discovers that from the top deck you can watch people spitting into litter bins.

Back at the Nautilus, Francis has been thrown into such a rage by his post that he has been forced to turn to his memoirs in order to forget, but his pencil is stopped in its tracks by an irritating stickiness on his cuff. Then he sees a blob on the front of his jersey. This is how it begins. A few food stains down your front and the next thing you know you're wearing boots latched with Velcro, strapped to a commode all the livelong day. He'd seen it happen to the brightest and best. He wonders if, unknowingly, he has become the sort of eater from whom others avert their eyes. Is it Rowena's curry that is shaming him? He jumps at the rap of his shell.

'Francis? Can I come in, or are you working?'

Rowena opens the door. 'Sorry, was that growl yes or no? Are you listening to the radio?'

'No, no. It's just to drown the silence of eternity. I've had a letter – they're giving that old tattybogle Scrabster a Festschrift.' Francis's eyes emerge, glaring under skewed spectacles as he pulls his sweater over his head. The blue vein in his temple is pulsating.

A what? What's a Festschrift? Some ceremonial Up-Helly-Voe sort of thing? 'Will they burn a Viking ship?' she asks.

'Wouldn't put it past them, but wrong island. How dare this cream-faced loon take it on himself to organise a Festschrift for somebody he's only known five minutes?'

Such a waste, going to all the trouble of building a ship only to watch all the painted shields and delicate rigging go up in flames.

'They want a contribution from me.'

'What, for fireworks and that? Or do they want you to go up there?'

'There'll be fireworks all right! A rocket up this poetaster opportunist – go up there? How could I possibly?'

'Still, I suppose it's nice to be asked?'

'A poem is what they're after, or an anecdote. I say, I don't suppose you could cobble something together if I gave you a few pointers?'

'Me? I can't write for toffee.'

A word jumps out from the texture of voices on the radio.

'Did he just say Heligoland? Are they talking about Heligoland?' she asks.

'It's where Strindberg spent his second honeymoon. With his second wife.'

Grinning skeletons in bridal veil and top hat in a dance of death on the rocky shore. A postcard of a painting by Ensor.

'You're not a secret wordsmith then?'

'No. Did they find happiness there, on Heligoland?'

'I imagine not.'

'But Heligoland wasn't the sort of place where people went on honeymoon, was it? A resort? Where anybody could just *go*?'

'My dear girl, I know nothing about Heligoland, and now less than I might have. It's always sounded desolate to me. Why the fascination?'

As he switches off the radio the inconsolable-sounding crying of gulls drowns the fading voices.

'Oh, it's just – a land that I heard of once, in a lullaby.'

A slice of honeydew moon on an ultramarine sky, a wedding dress and bouquet, top hat and tails whirling to the music of a merry-go-round; she hopes Mr and Mrs Strindberg were happy at least for a while.

'I'll just give the dictionaries a dust while I'm here.'

'What was it you wanted?'

'Oh, I've forgotten. It doesn't matter.'

She homes in on F, with a sick feeling of having chickened out.

7

The reception committee is waiting at a table set down on the foreshore. Celeste has opened a bottle of wine.

A green pickup truck crunches the shingle and two figures climb out, in bright green dungarees with a yellow stripe down the bib, and green and yellow Doc Martens. Celeste sees to her dismay, as she should have realised, that Natterjack is just a couple of kids. The girl squeezes the boy's hand as they approach.

'All right, Gus?' the boy greets him. 'Mrs Sylverstien I presume? And you must be Mr Sylverstien.'

'Oh, must I?' says Francis. He takes an instant dislike to the boy's rather rodent-like cheeky grin. The girl is quite pretty.

'This is Francis Campion the poet, Rowena Snow, and Gus you know, of course. Why don't you call me Mrs Zee. Tradespeople usually find it easier.'

'Pleased to meet you. We're Natterjack, obviously.'

The girl pulls forward the bib of her dungarees to flash the toad logo on the yellow stripe. 'Cos we're a couple of toads. Only joking. It's Nathan and Jacki, Nat and Jack, geddit?'

'Bungle and Zippy will be joining us later,' Gus whispers in Rowena's ear.

'Amazing building,' says Nathan, reaching for a biscuit. Jacki slaps his hand down.

'I've just realised who you remind me of in your jolly outfits,' says Celeste. 'The Color Kittens, from a charming book my children had but it got lost somehow. It was a Little Golden Book. I wanted to get it for the grandchildren but couldn't find it anywhere.'

'Very collectable now, the Little Golden Books,' says Gus.

'I designed them, the dungarees and the logo,' Jacki tells her with shy pride. 'Of course, Nathan's really the artistic member of the team.'

Celeste sees his green eyes harden but now she has identified the pair as the Color Kittens, she is all affability, inviting them to sit down and pouring them drinks.

'The kittens, Brush and Hush, made all sorts of wonderful colours – all the colours in the world,' she explains.

'Unbelievable,' says Nathan heavily. 'Which one am I?'

'Hush!' warns Jacki.

'If you come across a Little Golden Book called *The Lively Little Rabbit* –' Rowena begins, her voice heavy with some brooding resentment, but all heads turn at the sound of skittering wheels, and a crash.

Why me? Why am I the one who is tweezering bits of gravel out of a madwoman's knees? Need I even ask myself?

Izzie is seated on a kitchen stool. Rowena, crouching

before her, snaps on a plaster with more pressure than is quite necessary.

'Ouch! Sorry – this reminds me of my netballing days. Sorry to be such a nuisance. Not a very auspicious beginning, I'm afraid.'

'Beginning?'

Rowena empties the bowl of pinkish water down the sink and gathers up blobs of bloodied cotton wool with her tweezers. The madwoman drags a tissue across her eyes.

'Don't cry. I'm sure Gus can fix your scooter.'

'Sorry. It's just that I've had such a terrible journey. But I'm home now.'

She blows her nose loudly.

Rowena's heart lurches. 'Home?'

'As soon as Lyris Crane told me about it, I knew. I felt the Nautilus drawing me to itself. But when I met Celeste in Croydon, I'd no idea who she was, and then to find her sitting like some oceanic deity or presiding abbess in front of that pearly shell, it was like a vision, a waking dream that I'd waited for all my life and I fell into a swoon.'

'You did *not* fall into a swoon. Nobody falls into a swoon nowadays. Your front wheel hit the anchor's chain.' She lowers her voice to a gothic whisper suggestive of bats' wings flapping across the setting sun. 'You must leave at once. Now. Before it's too late.'

'How melodramatic! You sound like some ghastly horror film,' Izzie titters, but smoothes the Elastoplast protectively over her grazes. 'What on earth do you mean?'

Rowena can't say that this woman with her crazy

radiant simper has hijacked her own initial responses to Celeste and the Nautilus, and poses a threat to the balance of the little family of Celeste and Francis, Gus and Rowena. It is imperative that she remove her netball player's knees from Rowena's territory before they become fixtures.

'Gus will give you a lift in his van. Where do you live?'

'Near Sevenoaks, but –'

'He won't mind. We call him Mr Fix-it here.'

She snaps shut the lid of her first-aid box. 'You mean you scooted all the way from Sevenoaks?'

'No, bless you. But I would have, if necessary! Look here, I don't want to tread on anybody's toes but I'm sure you can find me spot to curl up in until we get it on an official footing. I've got my daughter's sleeping bag in my rucksack.'

'But she might need it . . .'

'Sweet of you, but this is her old one, a veteran of Glastonbury. A bit niffy but I can spread it over a bush to air.'

Rowena, sensing she is losing the argument, says, 'We don't do that here. There are rules about that sort of thing – spreading sleeping bags on bushes.'

'Of course. Every community must abide by its rules. You'll find me an obedient postulant, Ramona, is it? A willing pair of hands. I know you've probably been here for yonks and I'm only the new bug, but if you take me under your wing, I'll delight in adapting to your ways here and pulling my weight in any capacity, however menial.'

'Look, lady, there's no way you're moving in here.' Rowena picks up a pair of kitchen scissors. 'You can't just turn up out of the blue and announce you've come to stay. In the first place, this isn't a flaming convent. Second, there's no room at the inn, no vacancy. Third, we're about to have the builders in, and finally, you have to be an artist or craftsperson or at least some sort of intellectual to qualify. There's a rigorous selection process and a long waiting list.'

'All patched up?'

At Celeste's voice Rowena blushes scarlet as her hand drops to her side still grasping the scissors. How long has Celeste been standing there?

'Come back into the garden and have a drink. So you're a friend of Lyris Crane?'

They go out leaving a trail of laughter in their wake. Rowena slams her first-aid stuff, bowl and all, into the dustbin. Take a new bug under her wing? A cockroach more likely. Yonks. What's a yonk? A yeti crossed with a gonk? Lyris Crane. Interfering old witch, giving that ditz the claim to be on a social footing with Celeste. Is this Lyris Crane supposed to be famous? Lyris sounds like a tall white lily unfurling from dark green leaves. Crane: a symbol of longevity, a bird with slender legs extended, black-tipped wings dipping, long bill pointing south, a metal giraffe rearing into the sky over a building site. Hart Crane. Walter Crane. Dr Frasier Crane. Slow loris, whooping crane. She's never heard of Lyris Crane. Trust Celeste to come creeping up like that, and then be ostentatiously gracious to make up for Rowena's hideous behaviour. 'Look, lady,' she sees herself saying, jabbing the scissors like an outraged machinist in Mike Baldwin's *Coronation Street* factory.

As she is punishing the glass sink with bleach, Cliff

Waddilove hisses a warning in her ear. 'Mrs Diggins has got the 'ump!'

'I will not let that woman turn me into Mrs Diggins!'

She can just see Izzie trying to take over her kitchen, her darling Waring Blender, the KitchenAid, the knife block that is a cube of burnished steel, the blades whisper-sharp, not a rivet tarnished, the wrought-iron trivets, the bellies of good jugs and bowls, the books of recipes that she has yet to try. She has waited a long time to achieve a knife block of her own; the pine spice rack and mug tree, which had turned into time's laughing stocks, were as far as she'd got, and now that she was the chatelaine of a walk-in larder and a kitchen that was not only a design historian's dream but dazzlingly functional, she was not going to cede so much as a spoon.

Beside the knife block stands her pot of basil. In truth, Rowena is still a little nervous of the steel cube. No good ever comes of a knife block on television; her finger's on the remote ready to zap as soon as the camera glances off a cluster of sheathed blades, each offering a fatal handshake. She thinks of Keats's Isabella and the Pot of Basil. The pot is obviously much too small to take Izzie's great bonce. But just suppose. She imagines the scene: life at the Nautilus goes on as if Izzie had never been. But one evening, as Rowena grinds the finishing twist of black pepper on to a platter arranged with avocado crescent moons, the snowy whales' backs of mozzarella and cherry tomatoes with a fragrant scattering of basil leaves, she sees a single grey hair curled and glistening in the drizzle of golden oil. She turns. Grey locks are springing from the pot, strangling the plant, snaking over every surface, twining through cup handles, saucepans boiling over with them, a mass of living tendrils moving inexorably towards her; lunging, choking, dragging her down to hell.

The tea towel in her hands has twisted into a garotte. Get a grip. In the first place, she could never have eaten basil plucked from such grisly compost, and in the second, how would she have disposed of the headless body? In a Gro-Bag? What a delicious *insalata tricolore* she had constructed. She wrenches two hanks of her own hair until tears come. What's the matter with me? Oh, what is wrong with me?

A lifetime of loneliness and exclusion, her memory could have answered her, supplying any of a thousand illustrations; girls whispering about her in the long grass of the Chestnuts playing field, their hair mingling in a conspiratorial waterfall; the sight of a pair of teenagers on an escalator, eating each other's faces, his hand up the back of her T-shirt, hers in the waistband of his jeans; the laughter of the women at the Sunray Laundry; the restaurant waiter grinding a flourish of pepper over the plates of a raucous coven celebrating someone's birthday, throwing a merry 'Enjoy your mill, ladies' over his shoulder as he passes by the invisible lone diner at the table next to the Gents' toilet; the aubergine lips of Bernadette from Caring Options shouting false accusations.

Interweaving skeins of voices and laughter are drifting in from the garden; contralto, soprano, tenor, bass; an opera is going on out there, while Rowena skulks like a servant without a singing part. She recalls the sounds of children playing outside on a summer evening as she stood at the range in the Chestnuts kitchen, in the steam from two bubbling galvanised cauldrons; babies' nappies were boiling furiously in one of them, Cliff's white handkerchiefs in the other. She had a pair of wooden, copper-tipped pincers for lifting and stirring the cauldrons to make sure everything was thoroughly cooked, and for threatening the heads and limbs of any child rash enough to dart in from the game for a drink of water. Her fist clenches and she can feel the pincers in her hand again, tightening on Izzie's head.

She could slink up to her room; nobody would miss her. But if she does, Celeste will retain all night, maybe for ever, the image of Rowena out of control, threatening the visitor with scissors. Celeste must have thought *she* was claiming to be an intellectual. She has to get out there and superimpose nice Rowena on that termagant.

'Rowena!' Celeste is calling her.

How happy she had been earlier that afternoon when she went outside after the rain and the shingle was steaming all rose and cornelian and amethyst, and a rainbow dissolving even as it appeared. She'd sat on the breakwater regardless of the wet patch on her skirt and the scatter of raindrops from a tamarisk tree, playing fivestones with washed pebbles and scrunching specks of gemstones under her bare toes.

'Rowena!'

She blots her face on kitchen roll and, her heart thudding, not knowing if she has ruined everything, stalks out to join the party. Izzie's voice floats towards her: 'What a marvellous anchor. It's just like being at the seaside.' Still trying to be the centre of attention. Cosying up to the company as if the anchor's own chain hadn't tripped her up to tell her she wasn't wanted. Rowena can't meet anybody's eye. What has been said about her?

'It's worth a bob or two, if you should ever want to get shot of it, Mrs Zee. I saw one in a ship's chandler's bankruptcy sale in Deptford the other day,' goes Nathan Natterjack.

'I'll bear it in mind, Nathan.'

'You're quite like my great-aunt Lyris, you know, Mrs Zee. Must be a generation thing.'

Rowena observes Celeste giving him an old-fashioned look. His great-aunt Lyris?

'I call them the shoes of the fisherman, Natterjackie.' Francis is schmoozing the female toad, turning a slender crimson-socked ankle this way and that with evident admiration.

'Do you? That's really interesting. Nathan, wait till you're asked!' she reproves the green toad who is refilling his glass. 'Can't take him anywhere,' she adds with a possessive pat on his thigh.

'But I can't get over the extraordinariness of it, that we were all at poor dear John's retrospective and that Nathan should be Lyris's great-nephew,' Izzie gushes. 'It wasn't the happiest of occasions for me – my husband, Clovis – but that's enough of that. Fortunately, although I never thought I'd say so, I'm currently dogless so I've nobody to rush back for,' she adds, to Celeste.

'I used to have a little dog called Dandy,' says Francis.

Oh, wonderful. How long have I been here and you've never bothered to mention any dog to me but as soon as *she* arrives, you can't wait to tell her.

'More tea, vicar?' Gus pours the remaining drops into Rowena's glass without waiting for an answer.

'By the way, Gus, I don't think I'll be needing that scooter,' says Celeste in a low voice.

'I do apologise for getting your name wrong, Rowena.' Izzie turns her smile on full beam, the smile of a rational being placating a lunatic, as if it isn't the other way round. Rowena shrugs, mumbling an ungracious acceptance, not daring to look at Celeste in case she sees disapproval or even alarm on her face.

'Remember, Rowena, that you are only here on sufferance, out of the kindness of our hearts,' comes Wendy Waddilove's voice, 'and remember too that the world out there is full of dangers for girls with nobody who cares about them.'

'Somebody's got the hump,' said Gus.

Rowena recoils. He is the pits. No wonder – no wonder what? She doesn't have the faintest idea why a man like him should be living on his own at the Nautilus, but she is sure he is guilty of some crime. Now Izzie's rabbiting on about a ship's figurehead she'd picked up in Greenwich a hundred years ago. A bit saucy but great fun and going for a song, a shanty, ha ha ha. Yeah, right. People like her were always picking things up, other people's things, for what would be a year's wages for some. How much fun could a half-naked woman carved out of a lump of wood be? She should never have let Izzie out of her sight. If Lyris Crane is toad Nathan's great-aunt, she must be common, not a cultured or famous person at all. Not the type you'd expect Celeste to associate with. But who is, or was, 'poor dear John'? One more of *them*. Izzie is taking an olive, one of the green olives with a red pimento tongue for which Rowena schlepped to the Greek greengrocer's. Her hand hovers over the dish, a hulking cuckoo in the nest picking out the choicest grubs. Olive in mid-air, she stares at Nathan.

'It's vaguely coming back to me. Did you have orange hair? Were you that young artist with the orange hair?'

'"Were" being the operative word,' says Nathan bitterly. 'Don't get me started on the art world.'

'Don't even go there,' agrees Jacki. 'Mind you, Lyris saved my life.'

Et tu, Brute.

It gets worse and worse. God knows, Rowena had tried to be positive about the Nautilus restoration, even though she knew it would be hell having the Natterjacks around. They were tradespeople, she'd thought, and would eventually pack up their ladders and depart. Now their status has changed. Why does she feel such antipathy towards Izzie? She knows she ought to accept that the Nautilus was supposed to be a hive of activity, not a *ménage à quatre*. Despondently, she sets out, if not to sparkle, to be civil at least, in belated self-defence.

'Did anybody else see the rainbow this –'

The crash of breaking glass cuts her short.

'What the –'

Gus is on his feet, running in the direction of the workshops and garages, starting birds clattering in alarm in the undergrowth. Those kids again, Gus thinks, as he leaps a clump of seakale, but he is propelled by the thought that it is his own kids come to find him. Kizzy is wearing a cherry print dress, with bare brown legs and pink sneakers. Little Gus in denim cut-offs and an aqua T-shirt.

'Go on, Nathan!'

'What?'

'Go with him. He might need help.'

'Gis a chance, then.' Nathan pushes back his chair and, rubbing his side where Jacki's elbow has slammed into his ribs, sets off at a jog.

'Should I go?' Francis frets, then, grasping a bleached parasol that lies furled on the grass, crunches stiffly after the other men in his fisherman's slats; a gallant old knight in white linen waving his lance, thinks Rowena.

'Bless,' says Jacki.

'Mmm,' agrees Izzie.

Celeste narrows her eyes at Rowena. Joy floods through Rowena; they are united against these presumptuous, patronising interlopers. They are the Nautilans. She hurries to catch up with Francis.

Gus runs past his van, past a wicker picnic hamper and its scattered bits and pieces. The doors of Celeste's garage have been forced. Glass crunches under his feet. Somebody's been shot in the Wolsey. The windscreen is a mess of blood and smashed glass. All the doors are wide open, the boot gaping, the vehicle sagging on deflated tyres. But there's no corpse slumped over the steering wheel. The car is empty except for a lump of stone and an aerosol can of paint lying in red shattered glass on the front seats.

'Bloody hell . . .' Nathan stops in his tracks. Then, treading coarse glass diamonds into the concrete floor, he peers inside at the smirched walnut and green leather.

'Here comes the cavalry,' says Gus as Francis and Rowena arrive.

Then Celeste, Jacki and Izzie come upon the scene.

'It's OK,' says Gus, trying vainly to block the doorway with his body. Jacki shrieks. Celeste, her own face deathly white, grips Jacki's arm, staring at the car, at the face of her old friend with a jagged wound in his forehead smeared with dried streaks and drips of the blood that has pooled in her driving seat. Rowena and Jacki each take an arm and guide her to a rock, where she sits.

'It's not like they've even tagged it. It's just sheer – wanton vandalism.' Jacki's voice breaks on the words.

'The Philistines are upon us. It was beautiful, so it had to be destroyed. The Taliban are among us.' Francis is almost dancing with rage, whacking the ground with his parasol. 'What are we going to do about it? If I get my hands on those young thugs . . .'

'Don't panic, Mr Mannering,' murmurs Gus to Rowena.

'Take it easy, Gramps, you'll have a heart attack,' says Nathan, laughing. 'You going to report it to the Old Bill, Gus?'

'Of course we are!' says Izzie. 'When I was on the Bench –'

'I must ring Konstantin,' Celeste interrupts, rising.

'I'll deal with the police. Nobody's going to come out tonight anyway, but I'll give them a call in a minute,' says Gus who has noticed a condom and is trying to flick it under the car with his shoe before Celeste sees it.

'Leave that, Gus,' she says. 'Forensics might find it useful.'

They all stand watching as she gathers pieces of the picnic set, pale green cups, plates and saucers, knives, forks and spoons, glasses and drops them anyhow in the basket. She picks up a thermos flask and shakes it and they hear the tinkle of broken glass inside.

'Let's go back to the house.' Francis offers her his arm and, supporting each other and leaning on the parasol, they make their way to the Nautilus. 'What price the summer party now?' he enquires *sotto voce* of the stars.

'It's not as bad as it looks,' Gus calls after them. 'Forensics. She'll be lucky,' he mutters.

'Look on the bright side,' says Jacki, 'they might have totalled it, eh, Nathan? Nathan?'

Nathan's eyes are glazed, his mouth hanging slightly open. He reminds Jacki of somebody. 'I bet she had a carload of memories in this old jalopy,' she says softly. 'Poor Mrs Zee. Poor car. What a mess.'

'Yeah, but is it Art?' Nathan grins. 'Pass us the polaroid, Jack.'

It comes to her. Toad. That's who he looks like. Toad gazing at a shiny new motor car. But it isn't the thought of the open road that enraptures him.

'Nathan, no! You promised!'

But the lights of a Shoreditch gallery blaze in his eyes. The Turner Prize is within his grasp. He snatches the camera from the breast pocket of her dungarees. Poop Poop.

'Can I give you a lift somewhere?' Gus asks Izzie.

'No, no. I'm staying. I can help, give some support. I've done a bit of counselling. And I ought to be here when the police arrive.'

'Might not be a good idea to move in tonight, with Celeste so upset.'

'Absolutely,' says Rowena.

'And like I said, it might be days before the Old Bill come round. Where've you got to get to?'

'It's beyond Sevenoaks.'

'Only take forty minutes on the A21. Lucky they didn't touch the van.'

'Yes, wasn't it?' Rowena agrees.

Anything to take his mind off his stupid disappointment at not finding his children there. He'd imagined them in the clothes they were wearing last summer on holiday at CentreParcs, the last occasion they'd been happy together as a family. Only, he remembered, he'd kept disappearing to check his mobile.

Izzie looks from one to the other. Her shoulders droop. She capitulates.

'Who's Konstantin?' Rowena asks Gus.

'Her son.'

'Oh, *that* Konstantin. Of course. Silly of me.'

'Bye, Lizzie! Nice meeting you,' calls Rowena, waving as the van drives away.

'Izzie. With an I. *Au revoir*!'

'That's Liza with a Z,' says Gus mechanically.

'No, Izzie. For Isabel.'

The road curves past a pond set back from the pavement behind black railings and Izzie glimpses a heron standing on a reedy islet. *Why* didn't they touch the van? Gus wonders. Even if it wasn't worth trashing, you'd have thought they would have sprayed a bit of graffiti on it. The condom and the scattered cups and things; somebody had obviously been having a picnic. But who? He has a really bad feeling about the whole incident. After a pause he says, 'Got any kids yourself?' He tries to concentrate on what Izzie is saying.

'– daughter Miranda. She's in her gap year, working overseas. How about you?'

Gus envisages a teenage girl in khaki combats and a skinny olive T-shirt. Carole spends a fortune in Gap Kids. Used to. 'Sorry? Yeah, boy and a girl, Gus and Kizzy. Seven and five. Here, do you want to see a picture?'

'They're lovely. Kizzy, that reminds me of –'

'Don't tell me. Yes, they are lovely. Only I haven't seen them lately, since my wife threw me out.'

'Oh, poor you! That must be terrible.'

'I'm not over the moon about it.'

'We're in the same boat then, you and I. My husband left me.'

Silence fills the car as they realise they are in quite separate boats, rowing in opposite directions. I suppose I'll have to ask him in, Izzie thinks, I do hope he doesn't accept.

'Nice place. You're well set back from the road, aren't you?' says Gus as they walk to the front door, passing the weathered ship's figurehead which Izzie has recently cast into the grass.

An alarm rings in her head, faint as the tinging of a bicycle bell down the lane. What is she doing, letting a strange man into her house at night?

'Yes, but it's deceptive. We've got some very close neighbours. You know what it's like in the country,' she rattles on, fumbling for her key, 'everybody knowing everybody else's business, in each other's pockets. Looking out for each other. In fact, I wouldn't be surprised if the Hillmores, they're my nearest neighbours, don't pop round for a drink when they see I'm back. Lovely people, John's just been made president of the local gun club.'

'Oh, *those* Hillmores. She's big in martial arts, isn't she? Ex-army. Works as a security guard at Tesco's now, if I remember rightly. Look, I don't have to come in if it bothers you.'

'No, please. I'd like you to. You deserve at least a cup of coffee after your kindness.'

So it might have been that she was embarrassed into pleading with a murderer to enter her home to rob and kill her, but fortunately it was Gus. He reflects that she really ought to have the place alarmed, woman on her own, in view of the rising rate of rural crime, but thinks better of saying so. He's always being offered stuff from houses just like hers.

'Hello, Pongo.' He pats the head of a huge ceramic Dalmatian.

'Why don't you sit down while I make some coffee.'

She shows him into a pretty room with a low beamed ceiling, soft Chinese-yellow walls hung with pictures, and bookshelves. There is a cottage piano, an assortment of chairs, a gold velvet chaise longue faded by time and sunlight, and a painted grandfather clock with the sun, moon and stars above its dial. He chooses a bergère chair upholstered in a birds-of-paradise fabric and lies back, legs outstretched. Much more his kind of room than his cell at the Nautilus. A crackled yellow vase of wild flowers and grasses stands in the fireplace, and in front of the fender is a rug where a dog ought to lie when the fire is lit.

Why on earth would Izzie want to move into a ramshackle old seashell? She seems quite normal on her own territory, any ordinary middle-class woman who came into his shop looking for a decanter or something unusual for her husband's birthday. The room smells of old woodsmoke but he becomes aware of a brackish odour coming from the vase, and notices a drift of tiny dead leaves and pollen on the tiles of the fireplace, spiders' webs shrouding the logs and fir cones in the basket, a film of dust, mildew spores. The pendulum of the grandfather clock hangs motionless. There is no message from her daughter winking on the answerphone.

'Here we are. I'm sorry – it's a bit chilly in here.'

Izzie puts a tray down on the low table beside his chair, moving lumps of amethyst and rose quartz to make room. 'There are some biscuits, or I could make you a sandwich. I'm afraid there's not much choice –'

'No, you're all right.' Gus takes a couple of biscuits. Larder's probably bare. Not looking after herself, with nobody to cook for. She's quite thin under the baggy clothes, arranging herself on a rocking chair.

'So . . .' Everything he thinks of saying might sound threatening, intrusive or suggestive, the two of them alone in this room with the moon shining through the window. He notes that she hasn't pulled the curtains. 'Lovely house.'

'It was. It was a lovely family house,' Izzie hears herself blurt out. 'A happy house. Until I discovered my husband was in love with somebody else. He's with another woman now. Her name's Candy, of all things. She's really a high-class tart, if you call being the mistress of a disgraced Tory MP, as she used to be, high class. The funny thing was, when I met her, I found I couldn't hate her.'

'Heart of gold?'

''Fraid so. She's responsible for that ghastly Dalmatian.'

'So what's he do, your ex?'

'Potters about. Goes to book sales. He's got a fusty old bookshop in Maida Vale.'

'Sounds like my kind of guy. I mean, being in the same sort of game myself, workwise. You've got some nice pieces here. If you want to be shot of the dog, I don't mind taking it off your hands. For a fair price, of course.'

'I'll think about it. I've – I've got used to it being around.'

'Bit of company,' Gus agrees.

'Well, hardly!' She blushes.

'Or I could pick you up another one. Pongo and Purdey, what do you think?'

'Oh – enough about me. Tell me about you.'

'Could be a bit risky, having a pair. You might end up with 101 ceramic puppies on your hands. Me? What's to tell – I'm afraid it puts me in the same category as your old man. The old story – playing away from home, defaulting on the mortgage – you know the sort of thing . . . don't know what you've got until you lose it.'

Izzie knows of it only too well from her experience on the Bench, and in the lamplight she sees what nobody at the Nautilus has been allowed to: a spasm of pain and, yes, shame twist Gus's features.

'I'm so – so . . .'

'Lonely?' she says gently. 'You were right, about the

Dalmatian being company. Some days I think I shall literally *die* of loneliness.'

Gus straightens the rug that his feet have rucked, watched by her photographs on a shelf.

'I should've gone to my old man for help and then we wouldn't be in this situation. My wife, Carole, moved in with her parents at first but that didn't work out and she got a place through knowing someone in the Housing Department. I wish I had gone to my dad now – my kids growing up in some grotty flat on a sink estate – but I couldn't face him being right as usual. Pride, eh, it's got a lot to answer for. I guess I just wasn't enough of a man to eat humble pie.'

'Don't – don't beat yourself up over it . . .'

How trite and lame her words sound, as if she's some sort of counsellor fobbing off a client. She had been going to say, 'Don't cry.' Perhaps she should have.

'Why not? Anyway, you're tired. You've had quite a day, I guess. I'd better get on the road.' He stands up. 'Thank you for the coffee. Look after yourself.'

'Here, take some biscuits for the journey.' She tips the biscuits into a paper napkin and awkwardly hands him a little parcel.

Quite a day, quite a day. Being lost, the wait at the bus stop, Titchy, the horrible girls on the bus, that deranged Rowena, all of them hating her, the Nautilus, falling off her scooter, the wrecked car, all that red paint like blood, walking up the path in darkness with Gus. The truth is, she hasn't spoken to her neighbours the Hillmores for years. Avid hare-coursers both. All the moles from their garden have fled to hers. She won't miss anybody when she moves into the Nautilus. Even her agoraphobic friend Beth has become something of a burden with her querulous demands for lemon reamers and suchlike. It will do her the world of good to have to get her own shopping. Fragments of the day swirl round her mind. She'd never had this kind of day until she'd been alone in the world. What is Miranda doing now? Sleeping peacefully in her goosedown bag? She sits on, staring through the uncurtained window, while her grazed knees stiffen under Rowena's Elastoplast.

8

In the morning Francis comes into the kitchen, wearing his old brown dressing gown, to find Rowena reading a *New Statesman* she found in the garden. She has just realised that another disadvantage of the post coming at all hours might be that the others will notice that there's never any for her.

'Quite a night, eh? By the way, Rowena, I've got to go into town on Thursday, for the DAMS AGM,' says Francis. 'There's a reception afterwards, and I wondered if you'd care to come as my guest?'

'I don't know. It's rather short notice. I might have a previous engagement.'

'Don't look so alarmed, it was just an idea. Thought it might amuse you, but of course if you've got something better to do.'

'No. I mean, nothing I can't cancel. But what about Celeste, shouldn't you ask her?'

'I took her once and she was bored to sobs. Besides, she's still waiting for the police to call.'

'What exactly is it? I know what an AGM is, of course, but I've never actually been to one.' And at the only receptions she'd attended she'd worn a white cap and apron and offered canapés on a silver tray to people with no manners.

'It's actually SIPS, the Society for Indigent Poets, an

organisation which assists poets and their dependants who've fallen on hard times. Affectionately known as DAMS – the Despondency and Madness Society, as in Wordsworth. I've just completed a stint on the committee for my sins.'

One sin is weighing on Francis. A few days earlier he'd read the obituary of a reprobate whose request for yet more funds had been rejected. Unwittingly, in voting to turn down the deceased, he had refused a dying man's last request. Surely that was unforgivable? A contravention of every moral code. Wasn't there even a parable called 'The Importunate Friend'? He attempts to grant himself absolution, for he'd no idea the importunate one would call the committee's bluff by dying on them. But we know not the day nor the hour. His address book is filled with the names of the dead. His old friend Vivian Violett the poet, to pick but one, a former DAMS stalwart felled by a pair of antiquated ice skates. He must write to Magnus before it's too late and he finds himself writing yet another letter of condolence to a widow.

'But, what will happen there?'

'Oh, all will be revealed in the dullness of time. A bit of speechifying and then general jollification. So you'll come? Splendid.'

He hasn't been into town since the milk incident and, secretly, he's scared of venturing out alone on public transport and he can't afford taxis there and back. With Rowena on his arm he will not be invisible or a target of scorn, nor will he be flung to the floor by the jolting of the bus.

'OK. I'd better get on now.'

'Looks as if the snails have been at that *Staggers*.'

'Staggers?'

'*Staggers and Naggers*. The *New Statesman*. Somebody's evidently found it food for thought.'

'Oh, yes, *Staggers*. It's ancient, I found it in the garden.'

Rowena sits paralysed on the edge of her bed, mentally raking through her wardrobe, shifting hangers along the rail, rejecting the garments that hang there and taking out a series of amorphous imaginary ensembles that would transform her into the person who could walk into that terrible room. Now it yawns like a dark cave, now she sees a ballroom brilliantly lit by chandeliers where clusters of elegant, willowy poets fall silent and stare scornfully as she enters. She reaches for Angus who is lying on the pillow. 'You're no help,' she tells him. 'It's all right for you, in your blue velvet suit.' If she had something silky in the colours of her rainbow duster, something bohemian, a boa even, a shimmering top, or a chic, structured little suit with a smooth pelt, in turquoise or coral and matching kitten-heeled shoes; black crêpe trousers with a drape or cigarette pants with a beautiful white shirt of antique lace. Maybe she'll just wear her jeans, with a pair of yellow rubber Marigolds concealing her dishpan hands, or opt for the pink elbow-length pair she keeps for clearing leaves from the outside drains.

'And what do you do?' She dreads somebody will ask her.

'Oh, a bit of hoovering, laundry – I'm working on a novel – a novel way with filo pastry –'

Perhaps she has time to write a poem or two, then she

could say she was a poet. Supposing somebody quizzes her on poetry. About Sylvia Plath, for example. Would she have to admit she didn't get some of the poems? What exactly was Daddy You Bastard's Crime? Just dying on Sylvia, or was he actually a Nazi or something? She'd never call her father a bastard for dying, he was a war hero. Poor young Daddy, not much more than a boy. Technically, he'd made her into a bastard, but that was just due to circumstance. At least Sylvia Plath had known hers. That Ted Hughes poem about daffodils was lovely, but then he had to spoil it all by saying something stupid. She supposes she will have to ask Francis what to wear. And had she said previous engagement when it should have been prior? Oh, Staggers and Naggers! What staggers and naggers it all was, what a minefield, and she'd been looking forward to blitzing the chambers which had belonged to the two German ladies. *Donner und Blitzen, Gott im Himmel*, and she still hasn't got a new vacuum cleaner.

Later in the afternoon, Rowena's heart stops, then shrivels, when she sees a buggy parked in the hall.

'Hi,' says the young woman, in *her* kitchen. 'You must be Rowena. Were your ears burning just now? Celeste's been singing your praises. I was just making some tea, kettle's just boiled.'

She is so at ease in her cotton trousers and a loose T-shirt, bare brown feet on the floor, as if she'd walked in from the garden. So at home. She has short dark curly hair, heavy eyelids, an olive complexion tinged with rose and a wide smile. Rowena focuses on the baby.

'What's her name?'

'Evie. I'm Rachel. Apparently the police told Gus there was a snowball in hell's chance of catching the kids who trashed GranGran's car. It's so hideous. I just can't bear to think about it. It's not just the damage to the car, is it, although that's bad enough, it's such a gorgeous object, and between you and me it was an enormous relief when GranGran gave up driving – it's the –'

'Violation.'

'Exactly.'

'The place looks fantastic since you moved in, Rowena. I can't tell how relieved we all are that you're here. We've been worried about Celeste coping, rattling around in this great shell with only Francis who's as fragile as she is, but you know how stubborn she is . . .'

'I'd have said independent,' says Rowena stiffly.

'Oh, no disrespect . . .'

'And there's Gus of course.'

'Of course. But who really knows anything about him? GranGran's attracted some spectacular lame ducks in her time. I know you must be thinking the logical thing would be for some of the family to move back here,' she says defensively, 'but I just couldn't bear to leave the Heronry.'

'The Heronry?'

'GranGran built it for us. Well, designed it. Hasn't she told you about it?'

Then Celeste appears with a little girl who looks about five, in a green gingham school dress. She is hanging on to Celeste's hand with both of hers and planting fluttering kisses on it. 'I love you, GranGran.'

'And I love you, my precious, and always will – oh

good, Rowena, I see you've met my granddaughter. And this is Violet.'

'Tea up, you two. Where did we put that cake, Violet? Violet's made you a cake, Gran. Can you take Evie a moment?' Rowena finds the baby sitting on her own hip dangling a plump leg, scrutinising her face.

'It's got real flowers on it,' says Violet.

'I say, cake! What a beauty! I bet that came from a very posh baker's.' Francis comes in, rubbing his hands.

'I made it!'

The child runs to embrace Francis, almost knocking him off balance as he sings, 'Violetta, Violetta. Was there ever anyone better?' He blows a kiss across the kitchen. 'Rachel, you grow younger and lovelier by the day. How do you do it?'

'*Pas devant l'enfant – mon voiture –*' says Celeste.

Rowena looks from one to another. How cosy. GranGran. Celeste sits like a babushka, a painted Russian doll beaming at her babies, and there are more of them to come, a line of wooden graduated figures stretching into infinity.

'Milk and sugar, Rowena?'

Evie grabs Rowena's gold chain in both fists. Gently extricating the fine links from the baby fingers, Rowena takes a hand in each of hers and rows Evie backwards and forwards on her knee. 'Bluebells, cockleshells, Evie Ivy Over,' she sings softly, blowing a parting through fine hair the colour of a rich polished wood with ruby tones where it catches the light. 'Row, row, row your boat gently down the stream –' Looking up, she says, 'She's got a double crown. Isn't that supposed to be lucky?'

'Is it? How marvellous. You're brilliant with her. She won't go to *any*body. Have you –?'

'I used to work with children.'

'I could tell, from the way she trusts you.'

But I'm only pretending to be nice so everybody will like me.

'Are we supposed to eat the flowers?' Francis asks, extricating a daisy from the damp icing.

'We could put them in water. I'll find a little jug,' says Rowena and, still holding Evie, finds the tiniest and fills it with water.

'Perfect,' says Celeste and everybody agrees.

'I'm going to play the piano.' Violet runs off and from the bar comes the discord of a five-year-old improvising *con spirito*.

Francis winces. 'The beauty is in the ear of the player.'

'A little less bass, darling,' calls her mother.

'Let her play,' says Celeste. 'It will be shrouded in dust sheets when the Natterjacks start work.'

'You must come and see the Heronry, Rowena.'

'Thank you, I'd like to.' Preferably when the family isn't at home. Or maybe I'll come and commandeer *your* teapot. 'Where is it?'

'Herne Hill. And we do have herons.'

Francis pictures himself walking into the AGM with Rowena, to a hum of speculation; there's life in the old dog yet, they'd all be thinking. Then his fantasy is spoiled by the unwelcome image of an octagenarian preparing for the social highlight of her calendar, climbing stiffly into the sad black garments mothballed since the last meeting, crooking an insect-thin arm to pull the zip over fused vertebrae, brushing ineffectually at the white bird's nest at the back of her head, like a baby's hair when it has been lying in its cot. Her name is Belle De Groot, who once was *belle de jour.* She would be the first to arrive at the Chelsea headquarters of the society. Everybody, Francis included, had been in love with her; he feared she loved him still. Now she and her work were forgotten by the world. Well, not quite: Belle had appeared as a footnote in a recent Life of a less talented, in Francis's opinion, contemporary who was a household name, a critical biography written by some whippersnapper who hadn't been born when Belle was in her prime. The late Belle de Groot, said the footnote, was best remembered for her generous granting of sexual favours to the male poets of her circle.

Whenever he thinks about that footnote, Francis is thrown into a rage. Rowena arrives while he is still fuming at the calumny.

'So, are they *all* mad and despondent then?' she blurts out. 'I mean, will everybody be indigent? Who's going to be there?'

She was daring to hope that the DAMS would be a tatterdemalion crew in rags and jags.

'Well – there'll be the trustees and the committee and a general mêlée. It's hard to know who'll still be alive on Thursday.'

'Well, obviously the trustees and the committee will be quite smart. What are you going to wear? Will you be wearing your fisherman's shoes?'

'My dear girl, I haven't given it a thought. But of course I'll be suitably shod for town. Why do you ask?'

'Oh, it's just that – well, if you're intending to wear your pink tie, there's a spot on it. Oil. I could get it out for you with Vanish. Give it to me and I'll do it now,' she says, in despair.

'I suppose you might as well, but I've got dozens of others.'

She goes off with his tie, leaving Francis rather bemused. He gets out his brown boots and examines their crazed surface. Perhaps Rowena could bring them up to scratch. He's got a tin of polish somewhere. How sweet she is in her concern for what he should wear. A Yeats poem comes to mind. 'Shy one, shy one, / Shy one of my heart / She moves in the firelight / Pensively apart. / She carries in the dishes, / And lays them in a row. / To an isle in the water / With her would I go. / She carries in the candles, and lights the curtained room, / Shy in the doorway / and shy in the gloom; / And shy as a rabbit, / Helpful and shy. / To an isle in the water / With her would I fly.

Rowena, staring at her reflection in the glass, loops the pink tie round her neck. How easy it is for a man. If she had been born male, things would have been so different. But she would have been an ineffective little man, elbowed out of the way at bars, a duffer at games, a seven-stone weakling who gets sand kicked in his face, a failure with women. She thinks about that staple plot of soap opera, where a young man turns up claiming to be somebody's son. If only. But that could never happen to her; it is impossible for a woman to have mothered a child and not know about it. It is so hideously unfair.

The tentative hope rises that she might make friends with somebody at the reception. A faceless male figure in black. A rustle of bohemian femininity. A best friend. Someone of her own. A sneer plays over her face as she remembers the Dunlops setting out for some middle-brow Prom, while she babysat. Sheila in emerald and navy, and her husband sporting his birthday present, a blue linen blazer, masquerading as music lovers, looking forward to a tub of Loseley's ice cream at the interval. Even as she waved them off she had known that the real music was to be heard elsewhere, that her people would be listening to something atonal, dissonant and wild played on outlandish instruments.

Whoever she did meet at the AGM, she would avoid any married couples like the plague. They are always bad news. Either they present a smug united front or one of them likes her too much and the other is jealous. And they always close ranks. The Dunlops have a completed crossword puzzle, clipped from the *Observer*, pinned to their kitchen noticeboard; below the grid are the names of the previous week's prizewinners and, first among equals, highlighted in fluorescent yellow by George, are Mr and Mrs Dunlop of London SE. What a pair of losers.

But if she were to meet somebody, oh, the effort required to annex her life to another's, the wearisome explanations of years of existence. Any unattached contemporary would come trailing an extended family of adult children with problems and elderly relatives, while she had neither any achievements to offer nor a family to counterbalance the demands of his, or hers. Why should anybody consider for a moment getting to know her better? And if they did, the lustre lent by her association with the Nautilus would soon brush off. She doesn't really know anything about music; she's never even been to the Proms because she wouldn't know how to promenade. If only she'd just said no to Francis. She can't possibly go. She will have to be struck down by a migraine and spend the evening in her darkened room. She finds a pair of sunglasses and sets off to lay the groundwork of her approaching indisposition.

Celeste is sitting at the table outside, writing. She has weighted down a pile of papers with a large smooth pebble. At Rowena's approach she looks up, pushing her glasses to the tip of her nose.

'Good idea,' she says, noting the dark glasses. 'I should get mine. The light's so bright I'm getting a headache trying to read. It's very noble of you to go to Francis's party. Very generous.'

Rowena stares, forgetting to look sickly. This is a new perspective.

'Oh, I don't mind. What do you think I should wear?' she asks, casually dead-heading a yellow poppy.

'Your cherry-coloured jacket with the black linen trousers and black scoop-necked silky T-shirt and those mules. You're lucky to have such pretty feet.'

Rowena glances down at her set of brown toes tipped with cherry red. Sorted! Away with worries about tights and shoes. So much for a lady always wearing stockings in town. She'd known that jacket had her name on it as soon as she'd spotted it in the BHHI charity shop.

'Borrow these. Save yourself a trip indoors.'

She takes off her dark glasses and places them on the stone paperweight. Moving away a few yards, she sits on a cushion of thrift and watches a starling in the grass and two squirrels chasing each other round the trunk of a palm tree. She should go to the library and choose a book to bring out here, or she should make a pitcher of lemonade and carry a tall frosted glass, with a sprig of borage, to Celeste, or she could just sit here with the sun making coloured dots behind her closed eyelids, like the sheeny glints of the starling's feathers. She goes in to make to the lemonade.

9

Francis and Rowena set off for Chelsea under a goldenrod and foxglove sky. Francis is wearing an ecru linen suit with his pink tie and a panama hat, and Rowena is dressed according to Celeste's prescription. She supposes that the rule about never wearing brown in town doesn't apply to poets, and anyway the boots look right with the suit and match his walking stick; she'd managed to buff out most of the cracks. Gus drops them off at Crown Point, where they pick up the 417 bus, changing at Clapham Common. Francis has brought the stick as much for protection as stability. Time was, he reflects, when every old codger had the God-given right to prod passing miscreants with the tip of his walking stick or bring them down by hooking it round their legs, but at no point on their circuitous journey is he called on to defend himself or a lady's honour, or do more than poke the remains of somebody's takeaway from the seat to the floor. Even the bus driver, a comely young woman, vouchsafes him a smile instead of the usual hate-stare or contemptuous blanking.

On the King's Road he takes Rowena's arm to guide her down a side street. She feels a surge of happiness. After all her agonising, it's been so easy. It's so easy when you have somebody to tell you what to wear, and Gus calling after them, 'Behave yourselves, you two!' with a double toot of the van's horn. As the sky fades to violet, the pale globes of the lamps are waiting to be filled with aquamarine light when the last gold of the day has gone from the topmost leaves of the massy plane trees. She'd had no idea that the AGM would take place in such a pretty street with old brick and pastel-washed houses and wrought-iron railings and flowers tumbling from window boxes and hanging baskets. A breeze scatters a tiny shower from newly watered leaves as they pass. The evening is a watercolour still moist on porous cartridge paper with a tremulous drop at the tip of the paintbrush.

'What?' she says to Francis. 'Why are you laughing?'

Then she laughs as she realises she has been humming 'We're a Couple of Swells', and marching him along to its rhythm. Arms linked, both singing, they arrive at the steps leading to the front door of the SIPS. There is a blue plaque commemorating a painter who lived there once, and a discreet brass plate with the Society's name. No tubs of pansies bloom here but the entrance is guarded on either side by an urn holding a withered conifer. A notice, scrolled by age to parchment, reads faintly: 'Bell Broken. Knock Loudly and Wait Patiently.' Rowena feels a pang of disappointment at the premises, a frisson of returning anxiety as Francis grasps the knocker (shaped like an iron hand holding a quill pen) and crashes it three times on the black door. While they wait a pulsating jellyfish invades her ribcage.

The door is opened by a man with a tuft of beard on the point of his chin, and a smell of mildew rushes out past them into the warm air of the street. He greets Francis and holds out his hand to shake Rowena's and she finds herself presenting a frond of dead conifer, which she must have broken off in her nervousness. She follows them into a panelled room where her first impression is of a pair of cormorants huddling at the end of a row of chairs, and then a colony of various-plumaged birds descends and settles down noisily; she can feel their eyes on her in the light from leaded windows embossed with heraldic devices.

'This shouldn't take too long,' Francis whispers. 'They're all waiting to get to the drinks.'

Somebody switches on the candles of the wooden chandelier and the business of the meeting gives her the chance to look round at Francis's friends. So this is his world. The lady next to her rustles in her chair, releasing a smell of peppermints, mothballs and old face powder. Who is the greater poet, the dapper bearded one in the red suit or the one with flowing nicotine-stained locks, muttering to himself and clutching a plastic carrier bag, with an empty chair on either side of him? That lady in black velvet and beaded slippers; an instinct tells her there was once something between her and Francis. Her legs in black velvet tights are as thin as those of a gollywog her aunt made for Hamish, with striped trousers and google eyes. What had happened to him? But this is no time to be worrying about Golly, when she is in the company of so many poets. In her solipsistic anxiety, she hasn't taken on board, until this moment, what an enormous privilege it is to be here. She wonders how many of those present, sitting in rows of dandelion clocks waiting for the last puff of time, had once loved each other? Tumbled beds with bohemian fabrics, secret liaisons, broken hearts; Francis had never told her who had fought that duel in his palmy days.

All motions are carried *nem. con.*, the Lydia, Lady Yellenden Memorial Prize, for a self-published book of verse, is awarded, and the AGM ends with a vote of thanks to the stalwart ladies of the catering corps. Two gaunt ladies, sisters perhaps or friends twinned by long association, take a bow as the audience makes for the door leading to the refreshments. A small crowd is already jostling at the drinks table.

'Rowena, have you met –' Francis, returning with two glasses of red wine, begins an introduction to a tall figure who bends at the waist to kiss her hand, brushing her knuckles with his curved nose. 'Orlando Birdbiter,' he murmurs. His yellow eyes glitter under tufted brows. He looks as if he would bite smaller birds with that cruel beak, Rowena thinks, as he rasps his talons together saying, 'This all looks very festive. Let me find you a plate.'

At either end of the long table a grapefruit pierced with cocktail sticks sweats under its load of glacé cherries and Cheddar and around the centrepiece, a spider plant sprouting babies, is laid out a cold collation, circles of mottled sausage, chicken legs, twists of biltong, all sorts of curls and slivers of meat ranging in colour from beige to purple, to be served with silver tongs. There are bowls of cubed beetroot, a jug with a bead of salad cream hanging from its lip and another of celery, lettuce leaves and halves of curried hard-boiled eggs, cabbage and carrot coleslaw and a rice salad with chickpeas and sultanas, a dozen eggshells growing mustard and cress on cottonwool, platters of Kraft slices and Dairylea triangles, Twiglets, digestive biscuits and Danish blue, a ketchup-and-red-onion salsa with salt-and-vinegar crisps, saucers of Branston pickle, midget gherkins galore and tubs of olives; somebody had begun inserting walnuts in dates and grown discouraged, the remaining dates cling to their plastic stalks in boxes and the walnuts are mixed in with the peanuts and raisins.

Orlando Birdbiter hands Rowena a paper plate and a knife, fork and spoon wrapped in a Christmas paper napkin, and stretches for the chicken legs. As she hesitates, wondering what to take and how to manipulate her glass with everything else, the woman standing next to her remarks, 'Glynis was telling me that it's so much cheaper to get your nuts from the pet shop, and they come in these useful mesh bags. You can keep things in them.'

She picks up a torn orange plastic sack from the table and puts it into her handbag. She is bright-eyed and fluttery and looks as if she might exist on nuts and crumbs, hopping about on somebody's bird table, twittering little poems of thanks.

'Can I ask you where you are from?' she asks.

'From the Nautilus,' says Rowena.

'Oh. Well, I've come up on the train from Leigh-on-Sea, or Lonely-on-Sea as I call it.'

'A friend of mine comes from Canvey Island,' is all Rowena can think of to say, but her companion has darted away before she can tell her that the peanuts aren't intended for human consumption.

In marked contrast to most of the indigent poets, sprawled on a sofa in a corner, like a Regency cartoon character set down from a sedan chair, is a spherical fellow in a red-and-yellow silk waistcoat. His head is a pale dome and his vast legs, resting on an ottoman, are encased in nankeen trousers with a flap that buttons over his abdomen; he wears slippers on his feet. A procession of women is keeping his plate and glass filled.

'I say, can you move along please, if you're not eating? There's a queue!' comes a man's voice behind her. Blushing, she turns to face a tweedy poet with scraps of grouse moor sprouting from his cheekbones, and shuffles on, to encounter two women contemplating a fish with a cherry tomato in its mouth, garnished with swirls of mayonnaise and dill.

'Is that a trout?' asks the one in the gold snood.

'No, I believe it's a carp from the Lentys' place in Sussex, Monkspool. It used to belong to the Cistercians. Shall I broach it?'

'You know I never eat anything with a face!'

'It's barely recognisable. Go on, have a slice orf the tail end. I'm going to risk it.'

Rowena summons the courage to speak. 'I know this sounds awfully ignorant, but who was Lydia, Lady Yellenden?'

'God knows. Some amateur with more money than sense who died in obscurity leaving a small bequest to the Society,' says Gold Snood.

'I thought they might have given it to you this year,' her companion responds.

Rowena takes a few olives and moves away. Suddenly she feels desolate. I'm surrounded by poets, and I'm not having a nice time, she realises. Maybe it's her own fault, standing here like a dying duck in a thunderstorm. Though it's impossible to mingle when you're an outsider as usual. Nobody can sparkle in a vacuum. She tries a smile at a striking dark woman, but she is already turning away, presenting the back of an embroidered shawl. So much for meeting a soulmate.

'Haiku?' she hears Francis roar. 'Haiku? The haiku is the last refuge of the scoundrel!'

He is in a cluster of men, and a woman in a *décolleté* green dress who is obviously a *femme fatale*, throwing back her head and barking like a seal, and draping her arms round the aged *enfant terrible* whom Rowena recognises from the television. Such is the glamour of the box that she feels an instinctive thrill and urge to suck up to him, even though she actually dislikes him. The malodorous poet has taken out several more carrier bags which he had secreted about his person, and is systematically filling them; in go the curried eggs, platter and all.

Francis waves at her to join them, but she can't go over because she doesn't have a position on the haiku. Perhaps another glass of wine might help. On her way to the drinks table, she sees the man on the sofa beckoning.

'Are you a fellow-toiler in the vineyard, a new recruit to our merry band or is friend Francis to be congratulated on his good fortune?' he leers without waiting for an answer. 'I can see you're intrigued by the togs. Theatrical surplus. Only things I can wear in any comfort these days. Novelist's leg,' he explains, in a high, breathy voice, thumping a swollen knee. 'Contracted through years of futile labouring at a desk. Should have stuck to versifying but some damfool editor had the bright idea that I had a novel in me, and I couldn't afford to refuse the advance, pitiful as it was. Assumed the legs would deflate once I delivered the manuscript but it proved to be a permanent affliction, and then the buggers turned down the wretched book and tried to make me pay back the money.'

'I'm sorry.'

'Hmm. It's with publisher number eleven now, or is it twelve? I'm in the process of negotiating with the Society of Authors to take up the case.'

'Oh. I do hope they can get it published for you.'

'The case of the *legs*. The blasted *pins*. I'm suing for breach of breeches, heh heh heh. Would you be so kind as to get me some cheese and biscuits, and see if they've brought on the puddings yet.'

Rowena takes his plate, relieved to escape, and goes back to the table, where she tunes in to a snippet of sad news.

'Did you hear about poor Nadia? Got double pneumonia after going to a reading in Dorking. Nobody told her she'd been cancelled. She was left out in the rain.'

'I thought I hadn't seen her tonight.'

'That's because she's dead. Lucy Snowe, Francis's friend! What do you do, Lucy Snowe?'

Rowena realises she is being addressed and with the question she has dreaded. 'I – I'm a schoolteacher. Excuse me, I'm just getting somebody some food.'

She'd had no idea a writer's life was so fraught with dangers. Dropping a typewriter on your foot, RSI, paperclip and stapler injuries, painful paper cuts, starving in a garret, the usual hazards – but Novelist's Leg, and being left out in the rain like a poor doll, she'd never have guessed those. That creative writing class she'd signed up for once at Morley College should have come with a health warning. Particularly as it was where she'd met Sylvia Dunlop.

'May I advise you against the meats,' says a low voice at her shoulder. 'Some of them have been here since the inaugural meeting.'

'Oh, I wasn't going to. I'm vegetarian.'

He introduces himself. 'I'm Jenners Leaf.'

He is tall and greying at the temples with a longish somewhat melancholy face which makes Rowena think of a good rabbit.

'Rowena Snow.'

He doesn't look indigent, with long legs in black jeans and a grey cashmere sweater, and certainly not mad, though slightly despondent when he isn't smiling.

'Can I pass you anything?' he asks.

'What's in the sandwiches?'

'Grit and greenfly. Want one, they're delicious?' He gives the merest wink as he helps himself to a couple and Rowena realises that the beady eyes of a catering corps lady are upon them.

Taking a sandwich, she says, 'So, are you a poet?' She can feel her heart beating. 'Silly question, I suppose.'

'Not at all. Only in the most *amateur* way. I've done all sort of things. I ran a little magazine for years, used to print it myself, but – well – indigence was the end result. And you, are you a poet?'

'No, but listen, we've got a printing press at the Nautilus. It's huge and there are hundreds of trays of letters and fonts and things. It looked so sad, covered in dust and cobwebs but I cleaned it up and I'm sure it would work perfectly! It seems such a waste – all those letters just waiting and waiting to be put into words. We could get the Nautilus Press started again.'

'I remember the Nautilus Press,' says Jenners, smiling, but before he say can anything more Francis appears and takes Rowena's arm.

'Oh,' says Rowena, 'I've just remembered I'm supposed to be getting some food for that poor man with the legs.'

'Never mind him, sitting there like the Brighton Pavilion. Had enough?'

'I've only had one sandwich and one glass of wine.'

'Let me get you a drink,' says Jenners, taking her glass. 'Francis?'

He shakes his head. 'I meant, are you ready to go?'

Francis looks exhausted and frail. His face is the colour of his suit and the bridge of his nose looks as sharp as the beak bones in a bird's skull.

'Well – Yes, of course. I won't have that drink, thank you.'

'Can I get you a cab then?' offers Jenners.

'No, we'll be fine. Come along, Rowena.'

It takes some fifteen minutes of protracted goodbyes to get out of the room. Now, when it's too late, some of the women Francis introduces her to are quite friendly. I could have been talking to Jenners Leaf all this time, she thinks. I could have had that drink with him. She is starving. Scavengers are ranging along the table, filling doggy bags; some have brought their own Tupperware containers and Kilner jars.

'Call me, Rowena!' commands Orlando Birdbiter, who is very drunk. 'I'm in the book. Or you can always find me in Café Picasso.'

'Wait!' a voice pursues them down the hall. It is the woman who Rowena suspects was once involved with Francis. 'I want to give you something.'

She thrusts a baby spider plant, broken from the parent stem, into Rowena's hand. What does that say in the language of flowers?

'Belle, you mustn't take that hurtful comment in that silly book to heart. The fellow's a bounder who ought to be horsewhipped. But don't worry, I intend to set the record straight in my memoirs,' Francis tells her.

'What hurtful comment in which silly book? Who should be horsewhipped? I've no idea what you're talking about.'

'Oh. Do you know, neither have I! No wonder they call us poets mad. *Au revoir*, dear Belle.'

'Well, you made several conquests,' says Francis once they are in the street. She can't tell if he is gratified or censorious.

'Jenners Leaf is nice,' she can't help saying. 'He's – what's the adjective for like a rabbit?'

'Leporine. As in hare, but it's the same. Yes, Jenners Leaf is one of the good guys.'

'He has a leporine face, don't you think?'

'Taxi!' Francis is at the kerb waving one down with his stick.

10

For the first time since she moved into the Nautilus Rowena sleeps through her alarm and is woken from a grotesque dream version of last night's events by clanking sounds. Vague guilt and dismay, the fear of having made a fool of herself, chase each other through her mind. Jenners Leaf. She had told him he could use the printing press. Was that man's name really Orlando Birdbiter? Of course she'd never call him. But all those poets in that room; they must have thought once that they were touched with the divine. Surely they never expected to end up filling doggy bags at the AGM of the Despondency and Madness Society? Toilers in the vineyard who have plucked a bitter harvest.

She groans as she remembers a dream in which Celeste told her furiously to pack her bags because it is not a housekeeper's place to make free with the Nautilus printing press. Will Jenners get in touch? He was probably just humouring her, embarrassed by her gushing. What is that noise, that brutal scraping of aluminium?

She puts on her dressing gown and goes to the head of the spiral staircase. Two large ladders are propped up in the hall, along with planks and buckets. The smoke from toad Nathan's cigarette drifts upwards. Toad Jacki appears with two mugs. And Celeste's there with a plate of biscuits, chirpy as a grig, hobnobbing. Rowena retreats, slumps on to the bed and switches on the radio. It's a *Woman's Hour* phone-in on bullying; how could she have slept so late? Everyone will think she's got a hangover. She makes herself coffee, inwardly snarling at the thought of stained mugs, slopped tea bags and crumbs in the kitchen. It's a toad invasion. She has to get out. But first she must have a shower because her hair, like her clothes, is still full of cigarette smoke from the reception. She catches sight of the spider plant in the glass of water on the window sill. It seems to have given birth to several babies overnight.

'Rowena! How was last night?'

Damn. Celeste, carrying rolls of drawings and plans, catches her as she's sneaking out.

'Oh, it was great. What are those?'

'They're some of the original plans of the Nautilus. I thought Nathan and Jacki should study them.' She looks flushed and purposeful. 'Where are you off to?'

'Just a bit of shopping. We need to stock up on a few things. Tea, biscuits, kitchen cleaner . . .'

'But isn't Gus taking you to Sainsbury's tomorrow? Oh well, you know best. Now, what about the party. Who was there?'

'Loads of people. Do you know somebody called Jenners Leaf? I was talking to him.'

'Of course. Jenners Leaf is a *mensch*.'

'Is that good or bad? I mean, is he on the side of the angels?'

'Definitely. He was badly let down by his partner and lost everything. He had a little magazine –'

'I know, he told me. I was wondering –'

'Mrs Zee! Can you come here a minute?'

Nathan ruins the perfect opportunity to tell Celeste.

'I'm out tonight,' she hears herself saying. 'So it's *sauve qui peut* for supper.'

Celeste watches her go. She had been relying on her support today. She'd slept badly too, nervous about the Natterjacks, fretted by worries, unable to block out an image of a piece of bread thrown into a river and attacked by a hundred nibbling fishes.

'I see we're in for weeks of absolute hell,' Francis shouts down to her. 'Was that Rowena going out? A rat leaving the sinking ship. I was hoping she'd go to Crystal Palace for me.'

He'd fallen asleep during 'Sailing By' and woken at four, then managed only to doze before being roused by an infernal racket. A figure in green dungarees appears.

'Hiya, Francis!' calls Jacki. 'Mrs Zee, Nathan needs you.'

Francis would have been furious if he could have seen Rowena going into the Gipsy Rose Café, within walking distance of the post office where his parcel awaited collection.

'Hello, stranger, how's it going at the big shell?' Rita greets her.

Rowena is surprised that she remembers her. 'Oh, it's great, thank you. Only we've got the decorators in.'

'So you thought you'd escape for a bit of peace and quiet. What can I get you? Cappuccino and a nice almond croissant, or I could do you a *croque Madame*. Gus was in earlier, tucking into the Full English.'

'It's his fault we've got those Natterjacks swarming all over the place.'

On her way out she had seen a perky green pickup with their yellow logo parked by the anchor.

'Nathan and Jacki? They're a lovely young couple. I'm thinking of getting them to give this place a facelift.'

Fearing to put Rita's back up any more, Rowena opts for the cappuccino and croissant and Rita leaves her to serve her other customers, while she decides what to do with the day. The café is perfect as it is with bright green plastic vine leaves and tradescantias trembling in the breeze from the ceiling fan, jazz playing softly in the background and holiday postcards from regulars pinned up behind the counter.

She thinks about her first sighting of Gus here on a cold late spring afternoon. He came in, darkly handsome, in a borscht-coloured fur coat which looked as if it had once belonged to a Russian mountebank. The pelt of no known animal, it came down to his heels and was so bulky that he could hardly squeeze on to the banquette. It was a coat which demanded slivovitz or fiery shots of freezing vodka, a coat which had come from the steppes with snow on its boots, a coat with secret pockets which could conceal a pistol, a false passport, a pack of cards where the ace of spades appeared more often than it should, diamonds in a velvet drawstring bag.

Out of one pocket of that romantic coat he took an enormous egg and from the other an ornate gilt tripod, on which he set the egg. It was not a jewelled Fabergé egg which opened to reveal a miraculous Imperial miniature, the shell that Gus cupped in his hands as if coddling it into hatching, it was yellowish-white and pitted. Suppose, she thought, it did hatch, what if a beak were to chip its way through, and a damp chick stumbled out, or a phoenix flew up and perched in the plastic greenery, or a snake's head emerged from a circular hole, flicking and retracting a glistening tongue; a tortoise might totter out on uncertain forelegs, blinking as its soft carapace hardens in the air, or a snarling cockatrice or basilisk shatter the shell to fragments as it turned them all to stone. It could be a dodo's egg or an emu's or great auk's, or most probably an ostrich's.

'I pity the chicken that laid that one,' Rita had said. 'Got any more? I could get half a dozen omelettes out of that, no trouble.'

'If your customers would appreciate hundred-year-old omelettes. It would have been an ostrich. It's the biggest one I've come across. It's blown, look, there's a tiny pinhole here.'

When he spoke Rowena knew that he was not some flamboyant emigré slightly down on his luck, and he took off his coat to reveal an undistinguished sweater and jeans and drank a cup of tea which had never seen a samovar.

'Poor little thing,' said Rita. 'It does look a bit like an ostrich now you say. Pockmarked like the skin where the feathers have been plucked. It reminds me of a handbag with an amber clasp I nearly bought in the market, but the lining was rotted. You'll probably tell me I missed a bargain.'

'Probably not. You should trust your judgement – you've got a good eye.'

'Well, thank you, Gus.'

Gus. Augustus Egg, Rowena thought. She'd been

intrigued by the artist's name ever since she'd read that he was a friend of Richard Dadd, the Victorian parricide. The title of Dadd's painting *The Fairy-Feller's Masterstroke* always made her think of the unseen blow that felled her aunt on a green summer day.

A schoolgirl had come in, delicately beautiful, like a fairy's child, but evidently Rita's daughter, and appropriated the ostrich egg.

Rita remembers the occasion too. Rowena, as she now knew her to be called, had been in a few times before, always by herself. After she'd paid and left, Gus had asked Rita who she was.

'No idea. Just a customer. Why, shall I tell you were asking, next time?'

'Not at all. Just idle curiosity. Well, I'd better be on my way.'

He stood up to put his coat on, overturning the bowl of sugar on the table with his sleeve.

'Wherever did you get that coat?'

'Moscow. Or possibly at a boot sale at Virgo Fidelis. Like it?'

'The moths have been at it.'

'He's going to meet *her*, I bet. Lois the louse. I think it's horrible, when he's got a lovely wife and kids,' said Rhiannon when he'd gone.

'So do I,' said her mother. 'But what can you do?'

'You could bar him until he comes to his senses.'

'I've got a business to run. Anyway, he's a friend.'

She hated it when Rhiannon started going on about

families, and she grabbed a tape and shoved it into the deck. Chet Baker put the boot in with 'The Night We Called It A Day'.

'Go and do your homework and take that egg with you. I didn't notice your scruples stopping you cadging off him,' she said angrily, as if it were Rhiannon's fault that she was fathered by a Welsh hobbit in a field at a folk festival. She didn't even like folk music; she'd only gone to keep her friend Mariel company, who was going through a phase. Mariel was married to a consultant in Guildford now, with three children and two degrees from the Open University. She sent a computer printout of all their achievements every Christmas.

'Gus is a fool to himself, giving away his stock like that. He's his own worst enemy.'

'You're just jealous.' Rhiannon flounced upstairs, adding, 'Don't do me any dinner, I'm going out.'

Jealous? Of Rhiannon's having the egg? Of Lois, for having an affair with Gus? Never. She liked Carole and the children and she didn't want to see them get hurt.

Lois was one of those caramel fudge types; tall and fair and dressed in shades of blonde and brown cashmere, with gold chains round her neck and long boots and coach-built shoulder bags the colour of sucked toffees. Rita had watched her striding past the café more than once, her camel coat flying open over a pale polo-neck sweater, hurrying off to some liaison with Gus; she also had a fur-lined mac, and how pretentious was that? It had all started when Lois had gone into his shop looking for a birthday present for her husband.

* * *

But Carole and the children had been hurt. And Lois had dumped Gus the moment Carole found out. And Gus had ended up living in the Nautilus, with Rowena who, having finished her coffee and croissant is sitting there like two of eels, staring into space, in her little grey T-shirt and jeans and white plimsolls, with her little denim jacket folded neatly beside her. Two of eels. She'd picked that up from Gus. Even so, Rita thinks, Rowena looks somehow different. Before, she sometimes had that slightly weird expression that could make you wonder if she was a bit dysfunctional.

'Everything all right for you, love?'

'Lovely, thanks. How much do I owe you?'

'Have this one on the house. So, you've settled in all right? Do you think you'll stay there long?'

'Oh, yes. I certainly intend to.'

'So what was it you did before that, career-wise, I mean?'

'Oh, nothing much. You know.'

'You must've done something. Unless you're of independent means, of course.' She laughs. 'Or you've been away somewhere.'

For a moment, Rowena had wondered if she and Rita had become friends; the possibility of going on holiday and sending her a postcard had even flashed through her mind, but now she doesn't like her tone. The laugh didn't sound altogether friendly. What is this, the third degree? Away somewhere – like in prison or the bin?

'Actually, I used to be in the catering business – organising functions, conferences, banquets, that sort of thing, but I've been mostly in the caring professions.

Working with children and the elderly. I suppose you could call it a vocation.'

'Really? I wouldn't have guessed. Want another coffee?'

'I won't. Things to do, places to go, people to meet – but thanks anyway. How's your daughter?'

'Yes, she's good.' Except she isn't. She's started staying out late and Rita doesn't know who her friends are any more.

'See you then, Rita.'

'Yes, right. See you later, Rowena. Take care.'

Out on the street, Rowena finds herself walking towards Crystal Palace Park. She sits on a bench in the ornamental garden watching buses come and go along the parade. She didn't need Rita with her daughter and her complacent little café to point out that she'd wasted her life. How on earth *had* she filled all those years? Reading and mooching round galleries and falling asleep in front of the telly. Short-lived liaisons that came to nothing, with men she hadn't liked very much. Secret meetings with George Dunlop. She'd only imagined she was in love with him because he'd come on so strong to her when he drove her home after she had been babysitting his children, and she was so lonely. He was despicable. The irony was, it had been the idea of Sylvia's perfect family that she fell in love with. She and Sylvia had met at the Morley creative writing class from which they'd both dropped out, Rowena because she found that she preferred reading to trying to write, and Sylvia because George didn't really like her going out on her own. They had kept in touch, though. Sylvia was the only friend Rowena ever made on her cultural forays, and Sylvia found in

Rowena the ideal babysitter. Once in a while, to save face, Rowena had said she was busy, and Sylvia got quite ratty, as if surprised that she wasn't available at the drop of a hat. She made Rowena feel as if she'd let them all down. 'The children will be *so* disappointed not to see you,' she'd say.

When Rowena had plucked up the courage to run away again from the Waddiloves, it was in London, not Scotland, that she'd sought refuge. Chestnuts had ceased to function as a school, Mrs Diggins had long since taken the final hump, Belinda Diggins was engaged and Rowena was unpaid cook, cleaner and mother's help; the first set of Waddilove twins had been followed by another pair, toddlers now who pranced like spirited ponies in their reins on pale blue harnesses with bells on them, dragging Rowena through the deserted grounds, while beyond the tops of the trees was her youth, was rock'n'roll, was London, was Heligoland where her people were waiting for her. '*Bell horses, bell horses, what time of day? One o'clock, two o'clock, three and AWAY.*' She found a room in Primrose Hill and a job with an agency, and what bliss it was to clean those gracious, ordered houses after the squalor of Chestnuts. What joy to walk on Primrose Hill and Hampstead Heath at the weekend, to be watching a foreign film at the Everyman cinema while far, far away on the Waddiloves' radio *Sing Something Simple* tolled the knell of yet another Sunday.

Thereafter it was a slow drift south. How long had she lived at 15a Formosa Road? She couldn't even remember. Sometimes she's not even sure how old she is. She'd celebrated her last birthday with Pipe-Cleaner Man; for some reason she'd blurted out that it was her birthday, and he'd given her a miniature of whisky saved from his meals on wheels Christmas box. Rowena insisted on opening it and they drank a toast in the mid-morning twilight of his curtained front room. She still has the bottle, among her souvenirs.

Now she begins to agitate about her forthcoming birthday; should she ignore it, and hope nobody at the Nautilus will notice she never has birthdays, or tell them and expose her lack of cards? Could she bear to send a bunch of cards to herself? The thought of being the centre of attention, of Celeste feeling obliged to buy a cake, makes her squirm, but the odds are that one of them will have a birthday, and then somebody's bound to ask about hers. Bees are bumbling about in the salvias, pansies and alyssum; angst buzzes in her chest. I feel thoroughly discombobulated, she thinks aloud, and sees a vagrant, like a yeti or indigent poet, approaching her seat. There is no charity in her heart and she moves on. A sudden decision propels her to the bus stop and on to a bus, heading for the Caring Options Agency. Until she gets that sorted she will live in fear of Bernadette and be prey to Rita's innuendo.

The Caring Options Agency is on the ground floor of a purpose-built block between formerly majestic houses, one of which has been in a fire since Rowena saw it last. The upper storeys are blackened and it is boarded up, although an entrance has been forced through a window. The garden is scattered with junk and rotting furniture and tiny sycamores which have seeded themselves in the scrubby grass, and a cloud of flies hovers above a heap of something. Not a very healthy working environment for Bernadette; perhaps she will find her held at bay in her office by a giant rat. Rowena feels calm in her resolve, slightly distanced in fact, since she stopped off at Superdrug for those Quiet Life tablets; her first since moving into the Nautilus.

She rings the bell of the intercom. Characteristically, there is no response and a telephone is ringing unanswered. After some minutes the phone stops, only to start up immediately, and Rowena is buzzed in by a sleepy-looking girl.

'Yes?'

'I've come to see Bernadette. Can you tell her, please? My name's Rowena Snow.'

'She's with a client, and I'm on my break. You'll have to wait.'

She disappears through the door marked STRICTLY STAFF ONLY. Rowena sits down on one of the two chairs in front of the counter that runs the length of the room. The phone keeps ringing and is joined by another. Probably just some bedridden whingers moaning that nobody's turned up.

Through a perspex partition behind the counter, Rowena can see another Caring Options employee with her feet on a desk, eating a box of Kentucky Fried Chicken. Bunches of clients' house keys are hanging on hooks. The staffer licks her fingers and rings somebody on her mobile.

'You'll have to speak up, I can't hear you!' she shouts over the persistent ringing of the land lines.

Not to be outdone, Rowena takes out her own phone and pretends to check her messages. To her astonishment she is told: You have one message sent yesterday at 17.43 pm.

'Rowena? Remember us? It's Sylvia and George. Long time no hear. Give us a ring.'

In your dreams, Dunlops. Message deleted.

She can feel the jellyfish of anxiety writhing beneath the mild euphoria of the Quiet Life. The AGM. The Natterjacks. Rita. Now the Dunlops.

'Rowena! Good to see you! What can I do for you?'

Bernadette appears through the Staff Door. Patently there was no client. Her greeting is falsely friendly, as if she's got something to hide. She is as immaculate as ever, in a short-sleeved mauve linen-look trouser suit with black stilettos and a gold ankle chain, her hair as blonde, her lips the same glossy maroon.

'I've come to clear up the matter of Mr Apsley.'

Bernadette picks up each of the ringing telephones in turn and says, 'Caring Options. Can I just put you on hold? Now then, Rowena. Apsley, Apsley? I'd have to check my client files. What was the matter in connection with?' Diamanté chips flash on her maroon nails as she drums her fingers on the counter.

'You know damn well what it's in connection with, Bernadette. *You* accused *me* of stealing a hundred pounds cash from Mr Apsley and persistent pilfering of his petty cash. You were going to refer the matter to the police. Remember?'

'Oh, Mr Apsley on the Belfairs. Don't worry, it's all sorted.'

'Don't worry? All sorted? What do you mean, all sorted? Have you any *idea*? You accused me of stealing from a helpless old man. I had to find another job, without a reference. I was expecting the police to come round. I had to move out of my flat. How sorted can that be?'

The two assistants have come through and are standing with folded arms like bouncers outside a club.

'Need any help, Bernadette?'

'I was just explaining to Rowena that she's in the clear. A case of getting our wires crossed. The lady that took over from you, Rowena, she caught his son in the act of taking his pension money. Now, if you don't mind, I've got an agency to run here.'

The doorbell rings, and one of the assistants buzzes in a woman with a sheaf of time sheets.

Rowena stares from Bernadette to the burly, impassive bouncers, and rushes out into the street.

'Rowena, don't forget we're always recruiting for staff,' calls Bernadette after her. The telephones start ringing again.

Rowena sits shaking on the wall of the derelict house. She can hardly breathe. An empty earwig's carapace is lying on the stone beside her. It's Bernadette. She's hollow. She's shellac, she's Teflon. Nothing will ever stick to her. Everything glances off her varnished surface which is as hard as the diamonds on her nails.

She bursts into tears. How could she have lived in fear of that heartless sartorial disaster? She cries for shame for ever having been employed by Bernadette's dubious agency and for Pipe-Cleaner Man, who thought he had been betrayed by somebody he considered a friend, and then had to accept that it was actually Derek, his own son. She'd go round and kill Derek if she dared. The middle-aged slob on the bed in his singlet and pyjama trousers, smoking cannabis and following her with his piggy eyes through the bedroom door as she worked; she'd like to batter him with a Zimmer frame. It was Derek who reported her to the Agency, after Pipe-Cleaner Man had found his money missing. Poor little Mr Apsley. From now on she will give him the dignity of his real name. She hates to think of him at the mercy of a succession of strangers.

Then it hits her like a brick. She has left Celeste completely in the lurch. She is the housekeeper. It is her duty to supervise the Natterjacks. She is shocked by her total selfishness. She must get back at once. Should she ring? No, she'd better get a bit of shopping, as she said she would, and say she's cancelled her plans for the evening. There's a Greek shop near the bus stop where she can buy some of that dactyla bread that Celeste likes.

She is taking a tub of hummus from the shelf above the fridge when she sees a pile of bright scarlet peppers in clingfilm below. She could get some of those. Reaching for them, she sees to her horror that the packs are labelled 'Pigs Tail'. The red peppers are skinned pigs' tails oozing blood. She had almost picked one up. A woman, talking on her mobile, pushes past her, pokes at the pigs' tails and selects one, plonks it down on the counter, pays and leaves the shop without breaking off her conversation. Of so little account is the sentient being from whom this bloody portion has been hacked. Powerless and without redress. Sans voice, sans snout, sans trotters, sans everything.

Why do I live here, thinks Rowena, standing on the bus; I wish I was strolling down a pretty street in Chelsea, with Jenners Leaf. She should have made Bernadette apologise. She's read that anyone over the age of thirty who's seen on a bus is a failure. It's true.

The bus isn't moving. The driver's having a row with a man who's trying to use a child's bus pass. Weird that Bernadette should choose the same shade of lipstick as Mrs Diggins. It was horrible, Rita asking if she was going to stay long at the Nautilus, as if it wasn't her home. Wedged between two huge backs, she's fighting panic. She wouldn't put it past Celeste to go up a ladder. She'd found Mr Apsley on a stepladder once, trying to change a light bulb, and she'd just managed to catch him as he fell. Only yesterday Celeste had said, 'My friends are getting smaller. Not just my circle of friends, I mean physically shrinking, losing bone mass.' Rowena sees a huddle of brittle bones on the hall floor. The man with the child's pass won't get off. The driver refuses to go. People are shouting, 'Open the doors!' He does, and Rowena joins the scrum for the exit. She's got to get some air.

Out in the heat of the afternoon she thinks that she can never bear to get on a bus again. She starts walking. A taxi might come. Or she might take her bag of food to the park and never go back to the Nautilus, just lie in the grass under a big chestnut tree and fall asleep. And wake up to find this is a dream and she's a little girl at Chestnuts, with all her life before her. She'd get it right this time.

'Rowena!'

No. Please don't let it be. Rachel is waving from one of those high-up people carriers. She can't stop there but indicates and turns the corner into the next side street. There's no avoiding her except by running in the opposite direction.

'I thought it was you.'

Rowena feels hot and dirty, trudging along with her

carrier bag just as she did when she was an agency drudge. Both the children are belted into car seats. Rachel's hair is a mass of damp curls, Violet's in rats' tails and she's dripping an ice lolly down her swimming costume, the baby's wearing flowery padded pants.

'Come and have a cold drink in the garden, and see the house.'

'I can't. I've got to get back. Celeste needs me.'

'She'll be OK. I'll run you back. Hop in, we're causing an obstruction.'

Somebody is hooting furiously behind her. Rowena has to hop in.

'We've been swimming,' says Violet.

'I'd never have guessed. Wish *I* had.'

'You do look a bit hot and bothered,' says Rachel.

Unlike you, smelling of chlorine in your sleeveless linen top and shorts. 'There was a fight on the bus and everybody had to get off.'

'Poor you.'

For being such a failure that I have to use public transport, bringing a whiff of unpleasantness into your air-conditioned fortress of a car? 'Look, Rachel, I really should get back. Those Natterjack people have started, and I'm terrified Celeste will get up on a ladder and have a fall. I didn't realise they were coming so soon.'

'Here we are.'

Rachel turns into open double gates. The Heronry is all wood and glass with eaves sloping to the ground. Bushes and wild flowers grow in meadow grass on either side of the worn brick path. There is much fussing with seat belts and bags and library books and Rowena finds herself holding Evie again. The baby makes straight for her earrings and gold chain.

'Don't worry about GranGran. I've just spoken to my sister on the phone and she just talked to GranGran. She's fine. She sent the Natterjacks off to buy paint in the Fulham Road and they're not back yet. Let me get these two sorted and I'll get us a drink and then I'll give you the tour.'

Of course you would know better about GranGran, the wires of the Zylberstein family network buzzing across London as usual. What makes you so sure I'm dying to admire your brilliant house, and where are all the herons then? As they pass through the kitchen Rowena has the fleeting impression of a mountain landscape, slate, granite, ferns and cool running water.

'We've been here ten years now,' says Rachel. 'It's all pretty eco-friendly.'

Like I care. Just give me a Diet Coke. I need a caffeine hit.

The pond is at the end of the garden, behind a fence made from slender tree trunks, some of which have put out leaves. The Heronry hangs upside down in the water with a moorhen swimming past its roof among reflections of trees, bulrushes, great reed mace and drifts of willow and the hard knots of alder fruits and the buddleia lunging purple beaks over the surface. And there, up to the whites of its thighs in the water, stands a heron. Rowena gasps with pleasure in spite of herself. Rachel is beaming.

What is it about Rachel? Rowena wonders. This quality she has – is it of expecting happiness? They are lying in the meadow grass near the house, Evie on a rug, eating a banana, and Violet splashing in an inflatable paddling pool. The Diet Coke and home-made biscuits, as well as the heron, have eased her truculence and she could almost forget that she's in gross dereliction of duty. They have broken into the hummus and one of the Greek loaves; several fingers had been snapped off anyway in the crush of the bus. Rowena has rolled up her jeans, having declined Rachel's offer of a pair of shorts. She decides against telling Rachel about the pigs' tails; the story would show her in a dreary light, and besides it was too hideous; like the bushmeat she'd seen in Brixton Market, a monkey and a giant grasscutter rodent, the pigs' tails can never be spoken of. Until now, she'd managed to block out the memory of those pigs' ears her minimarket in Formosa Road had got in, for dogs to chew. She'd told Jimmy, the owner, that he'd couldn't make silk purses from them, but he'd just stared at her as if she was mad. It didn't matter, because she could never go back to the shop.

'Is that a Camberwell Beauty? Look! By the corkscrew hazel. I think it is!' Rachel points.

'There's another. It's a pair. Fantastic.'

Yet again, though, she reflects, I'm in an enchanted garden belonging to someone else, living on their time, admiring their flora and fauna. Then it dawns on her that Rachel is not showing off about the house but that she perceives Rowena as Celeste's friend who would naturally have an interest in her work, someone who cares about buildings.

'I once won a prize for making a picture with Butterfly Brand Gummed Paper Shapes. They were made in Camberwell,' she says, in a jokey self-deprecatory way. It is the first information about herself she has offered. It was the only prize she'd ever won, and she had thought that Camberwell must be a very beautiful place. Now, when she goes through Camberwell on the bus, she always looks out for the mosaic butterfly set in the wall near the shopping arcade, before Butterfly Walk, where a man was shot dead only yesterday.

'Brilliant,' Rachel is saying. 'Did you keep it up, go to art school? You and GranGran went to the Bonnard show, didn't you?'

But Evie, having finished her banana, holds out her hands imperiously to Rowena to be wiped. As she bends to obey, a peculiar swimmy sensation fills her head and prickles her eyes and nose. What brought that on? she wonders, removing banana from her hair.

'You say when you want to go. Or it would be lovely if you stayed to supper and met Paul.'

Rachel is holding up a bunch of black grapes, picking one off and biting it in half for Evie. I've got her on a postcard at home, Rowena realises; she's a Bacchus by Caravaggio.

'I really ought to get back. But you don't need to drive me, put the children in the car again. I'll get a minicab.'

'Nonsense. After all *I* kidnapped you. It'll be fun and GranGran will be delighted to see the girls.'

'But what about your husband – Paul – won't he mind if you're not here when he gets back from work?'

Rachel looks surprised. 'Of course not. He'll be sorry to have missed you, that's all.'

Does Rachel live in a world where everything is so easy and fun and sun and butterflies, or does she make the world that way? Rowena ponders as they sit in the car, stuck in traffic on Knights Hill, all singing along to a Fun Song Factory cassette.

The way she'd said 'You and GranGran went to the Bonnard', as if it was quite natural that they should. But Rowena had hardly slept the night before. Some friend of Celeste's, possibly the mythical Lyris Crane, had blown her out and she'd asked Rowena if she'd like to go with her. When they got to the Royal Academy, people who'd seen the show were coming out smiling, but Rowena was miserable. She'd trailed round after Celeste, standing in front of the gorgeous paintings in colours that looked like fruit juice soaked into the canvas, pretending to be a person who was at the Bonnard show with a friend, while all the time she was a monochrome housekeeper with no friends of her own, worrying about whether she'd be able to find Celeste a seat in the café afterwards, and angsting about the journey home, wishing she'd had the forethought to buy some Quiet Life. In the event, Celeste had taken her for tea in the Friends' Room, and she hadn't held her responsible for the delay on the tube or the long wait for a taxi at Brixton, but in her heart Rowena knew she'd been unworthy of the Bonnard.

Francis is sitting outside when they get back, with a notebook on his knee and a pencil in his hand.

'Where have you been all day, Rowena?' he grumbles. 'I had to go up to the Palace to collect that wretched parcel, and what do you think was in it? An Orkney cheese!'

Rachel and Rowena look at each other and laugh.

'Well, Rowena's got some nice bread, so that's supper taken care of,' says Rachel.

Nathan and Jacki are sitting in the bar drinking beer from the bottles.

'This would be such a cool place for a party,' Nathan greets them.

Violet heads for the piano, and Rowena follows her. She strikes one ultramarine note with a finger and then another, and realises that she is picking out a wistful approximation of 'Oh Where and Oh Where Has My Little Dog Gone?'.

They find Celeste in the library.

'I'm having my doubts about the Color Kittens,' she says. 'Nathan's showing an unhealthy interest in my poor car. Jacki's confided that he's got plans for staging a comeback, using it for some sort of installation. Photographs or a video, I think. She's worried sick. Just when they've got the business on its feet. And I gather he was never much cop as an artist.'

'Watch out, he's probably planning to have his private view in the bar. Any word from the police?' asks Rachel.

'I don't think they regard it as a priority. Your father's helping me sort out the insurance. Not so fast, Violet!'

The little girl is spinning round and round in a swivel chair.

'Do you remember Francis's little dog, called Dandy?' Rowena says to Celeste.

'Oh yes. He was a lively fellow, black and white with a plumed tail, and somebody else had a French bull terrier with a patch over her eye. She was called Frenchie. They were great pals, used to do tricks together, jumping through hoops and so on.'

'I wish I could of seen them,' says Violet.

'So do I,' says Rowena. There is so much she has still to learn about the Nautilus.

'When's your birthday, Rowena?' asks Violet. 'Mine's in March.'

'Oh, I'm much too old to have birthdays! Celeste, I changed my plans for tonight, so I'm quite happy to cook something. I'd better go and get on with it.'

She listens outside the door for a moment to hear what they are saying about her, but it is quite soundproof.

'I'm pleased you and Rowena have made friends. I know she's older and you have a busy life, but you seem to hit it off,' is all Celeste says.

It seems to her that Rowena has missed out on three vital stages of building a life and lasting friendships; family, a proper school and university. She has pieced together bits of her history, and her blood boils at the thought of those Waddiloves, who called themselves progressive teachers. If they had stolen the education and blighted the confidence of one bright little girl, how had they betrayed the other orphans in their care and the *Kinder* of refugees and internees?

'GranGran? You're miles away.'

'I was just thinking about friends of mine and your grandfather's who were interned as enemy aliens during the war, on the Isle of Man. And sent to camps in Australia too.'

'Oh.'

Her grandmother has an album of photographs which

she keeps hidden away. When Rachel had found them, as a child, Celeste had said, '"Whereof one cannot speak thereof one must be silent." We'll talk about them one day.' But they hadn't yet.

Weren't some of the ships carrying internees torpedoed? she wants to ask.

'Shall I ring Paul and tell him to come over? I could give Rowena a hand in the kitchen.'

'Yes, why don't you? Try to find out when her birthday is.'

11

Gus did not appear for the evening meal but the following day at six o'clock he is waiting to take Rowena to Sainsbury's. He slips in the pound coin and releases the trolley with a practised hand.

'Do you want to push or shall I?'

'I'd rather, but you don't have to come round with me if you'd rather wait in the café.'

'No, it's OK. I can pick up some things for myself.'

'I'm not really familiar with the layout of this branch. It's vast, isn't it?'

'Have you got a list? We'll do the heavy stuff first and come back for the fruit and veg.'

Rowena finds herself shopping at a faster pace than she'd imagined, rather than browsing along taking her time to look and make impulse purchases of things they don't really need. Is this what being married's like? She'd always envied couples shopping together, thinking that it must be so nice to have somebody to do the boring, routine things with, to plan meals together, just to be able to turn to someone and say 'Shall we have this one or that one?'

It is a long time since she's done a really big shop. Most of her clients at Caring Options had their stuff delivered weekly by an agency, but she used to pick up odd items for them at their corner shops, milk, bread, cat food, small tins of fruit cocktail in heavy syrup and macaroni cheese and so on. She collected their pensions from the post office. Now that the fear has gone, she can allow herself to think about her clients; she'd gone round to say goodbye to them all, except Mr Apsley of course, after Bernadette had fired her. She was appalled that he believed she would steal from him, especially after they had shared the whisky on her birthday like friends.

It had been so terrible, Bernadette coming round to her flat and making her hand over all her clients' keys. Such humiliation. Bernadette was shouting and she'd been sure the neighbours could hear her strident accusations. 'You haven't heard the last of this!' was her parting shot, and Rowena crashed the front door so hard that all the windows in the house shook. She expected the other tenants to come rushing out but there was a deathly silence, as if they'd all been listening to every word. She was branded a thief in her own house. Rowena was in anguish, yes that was the word, anguish, pacing and wringing her hands. She wanted to scream her innocence, cry in somebody's arms and be comforted, and have somebody to fight for justice on her behalf, but she had nobody to turn to. She was so tainted that she could not speak to Sylvia, who anyway had always despised her job. Eventually, she went to bed and stayed there for days lying like a stone watching television; she felt she'd crossed a divide, so that when shows like *Kilroy* and *Trisha* came on, she was one of those people who had done awful things. She felt their shame as her own.

Rowena had thought that Gus would be the only person she could tell about the affair, that she might tell him tonight and she'd even fantasised about him striding into the Caring Options building to confront Bernadette, and driving to the Belfairs Estate to land a punch on Derek Apsley's stubbly chin. But Gus is preoccupied, grazing absent-mindedly on a bag of crisps. So it's business as usual; she might as well be doing the shopping by herself. She bets it isn't like this when Rachel and Paul go to Sainsbury's; they would be arguing amicably over the organic vegetables, debating which gourmet vinegar to try and selecting the right wine to complement the meal they were going to cook together. Paul wouldn't stalk round silently, bunging things into the trolley as if he couldn't wait to get out, like Gus. Paul was lovely, tall and a bit rotund, with gingery curly hair and glasses, and he and Rachel didn't give her the uneasy feeling that most couples did, as if one of them might turn. She tries to picture herself shopping with Jenners Leaf, his leporine face smiling at her as she picks out a lettuce.

This is crazy, going round a supermarket with Rowena, Gus is thinking. What am I doing here? Where's Carole? All around them tiny babies are sleeping in trolley baskets, toddlers strapped into seats are grabbing things off the shelves, kids are driving their parents mad. He is tempted to abandon Rowena and their heaped trolley in the middle of the aisle and run out of the shop, like a bridegroom leaving the bride at the altar.

'All done, then?' he says, making an effort. It isn't her fault and he did offer to take her.

She nods.

'I'll take the trolley now, then. It's heavy.'

'OK.'

'Heard any more from whatsername, Izzie with the scooter?'

'No. She hasn't been in touch. Perhaps she's changed her mind. I hope so.'

'She's not so bad really, once you get to know her. Not that I do, but she's different on her own home ground.'

Why doesn't she stay there then? Rowena is suffering checkout angst now, the fear of not being able to unpack and pack all this shopping quickly enough. She is hoping there will be somebody to pack for her. There isn't, but Gus proves to be a professional.

Gus remembers Izzie giving him the biscuits for his journey. That was very sweet. She's got that lovely house with a big garden and an adjoining paddock, where you could graze a couple of ponies. His children are living in a block of flats with a notice saying 'No Ball Games' and a dangerous-looking adventure playground.

When they get home he helps to carry in the bags and then says he's going to meet some mates. Rowena has none of the pleasure she had anticipated in putting away the shopping; it is just a chore. She goes to rinse out the common mugs she has bought for the Natterjacks to use and finds one of the glass sinks blocked by a J-cloth that smells of white spirit and a Pot Noodle filled with used tea bags. Celeste has gone out and Francis is in his room, probably working on that Festschrift poem which has put him in such a bad mood. That leaves Angus for company. Funny that Jenners should have the same name as the shop in Edinburgh where they'd bought

Angus. She is relieved now that she didn't embarrass herself by telling Gus about Bernadette, and blushes to think she'd imagined him as a knight in shining armour. So much for Mr Fix-it. How absurd that she'd ever mistaken him for a romantic Russian, and secretly named him Augustus Egg.

Gus feels out of place again in the restaurant, sitting at a table with the three men, acquaintances rather than real mates, he'd met up with in the pub. They are all in their shirtsleeves, guffawing to show they are blokes out having a good time, and he can't get on their wavelength tonight. Next to them, two tables have been pushed together to accommodate a family party who are enjoying the seafood platter topped with a lobster, piling up the mussel shells on their sideplates like heaps of discarded blue slippers. In the corner, Nathan's parents, Buster, the Floral King of the South-East, and his lady wife Sonia, are having dinner *à deux*; the waitress is carrying a tray of liqueurs to their table. The ritual of the flaming coffee bean. Sonia has seen him and lifts her glass in greeting. Gus sneaks a look at his watch.

'It's five minutes later than the last time you looked,' says Andy. 'Are we keeping you up?'

'Sorry, guys. Things on my mind.'

They all, Andy, Tom and Stuart, nod sympathetically, but Gus stands up and puts some notes on the table.

'You'll have to excuse me, I'm not very good company at the moment. I'll catch up with you later, OK?'

On his way to the side road where he's left the van,

Gus walks past the closed Gipsy Rose Café, and finds Rita in the doorway, looking down the street. Her hair is sticking up as if she's been raking her fingers through it, her face looks pale and sweaty under the light and she's wearing a sleeveless cotton shift dress and old espadrilles.

'You haven't seen Rhiannon, have you?'

'No. Why, has she gone missing?'

'Not really. It's just that it's getting late and I don't know where she is. I never know where she is nowadays or who with, and I think she might be bunking off school sometimes. The thing is, she's upset. She had a letter from her father and she doesn't know if she wants to see him or not after all these years. Of course, *I* don't want her to, but it has to be her decision. I wish you'd talk to her, Gus. She respects you. She looks on you as a sort of father figure. I suppose you have been more of a father to her than he has.'

Leave me alone, Gus thinks. I'm not even a father to my own children, or a husband to my wife.

'I'll have a word. Give us a bell if she doesn't turn up.'

At that moment a group of teenagers, Rhiannon among them, comes noisily round the corner.

'OK, then, Reet? Good luck. See you in the morning, I expect.'

He sits in the van and rings Carole's number. Her phone is switched off but he leaves a message. 'Carole, it's me. We've got to get this sorted out. I can't stand it much longer. I'll find us a decent place to live if you'll just say we can make a fresh start, in fact I'm working on it now. I miss you all so much and I love you. I'm begging you, Carole, please call me. I'm sorry, sorry, sorry, sorry . . .'

Lying on his bed waiting for the phone call which won't come, Gus shuts his eyes, thinking that he'd never seen Rita looking so scruffy and down-trodden before; it was as if he'd glimpsed the secret Rita inside the professional daytime personality that she took off and hung up like a uniform as soon as the sign on the café door was turned round to CLOSED.

And Rowena in Sainsbury's. She'd had a closed, unhappy expression that was somehow familiar and reminded him of the face of somebody much younger. At once, he sees two ladies under a tree, sewing white material. He's crying. Is he lost? He's only a little boy, two, three? He's fallen over and hurt his hands and knees on prickly things in the grass. The ladies are cross with each other but the younger one, the girl, he can see now that she is a girl although then she was like a grown-up to him, has a brown face and black hair in a fringe and dark eyes. She takes his hand and leads him back through the long grass to a big house and Dad's there and swings him up on to his shoulders. He is sure the girl is Rowena.

He screws up his eyes tightly, concentrating, trying to focus on the picture of the little boy crying and the two ladies but it fades, leaving him with the memory of a desolate sense of loss, of being alone in a great wide world. There was another man with Dad, he thinks, and some big children. Was it a school? But what were he and his father doing there? It must have been some job Dad was on. So that was where he had seen Rowena before, not Whiteladies. A good thing he'd never got round to asking her about that, but now he could get her to piece it all together.

Carole obviously has no intention of returning his call, so he rings her again and leaves another message.

Rowena is walking back, swinging an empty basket, from the washing lines, which are screened off at the side of the building, when she sees Gus going towards his van. He has been parking it in the drive since the attack on Celeste's car.

'Guess what? I've just discovered a swimming pool,' she greets him.

'No. Where?'

'Behind the studios. I'd never been there before because it's so overgrown, and there it was.'

'With water in it?'

'Only a bit of rainwater and dead leaves, but I bet we could get it going again. Wouldn't that be fabulous? It's quite small, with green tiles.'

The awkwardness of the previous evening is dissolved by her enthusiasm, and it's a beautiful clear morning with the moisture in the air not yet burned off by the sun.

Gus describes his memory of the ladies sewing under the tree. 'Does it ring any bells? Could it have been your boarding school and could that young girl have been you? She was in her teens, I guess. Do you remember a little boy who was crying?'

'There were always little boys crying. Yes, I think I do remember vaguely. There was some sort of electrician or something –'

'That was Dad!'

'But I thought you lived on Canvey Island. It seems a long way to come.'

'It must have been some sort of specialist job. Dad had a very high reputation and he was in demand to travel all over.'

'Anyway, this man did have a little boy with him. He had his own little set of tools.'

'That was me. That was definitely me. And that was you. Gordon Bennett!'

Rowena sits down on a log and watches him driving away. I've got a shared history, she thinks. It may be only a fragment, but after all these years, I've got a shared past.

She finds Celeste sitting outside with a pot of coffee, opening her post.

'Guess what, I've got a shared past, with Gus. Isn't that extraordinary?'

'Get yourself a cup, and tell me about it.'

'Oh, and I've discovered a swimming pool.'

When she comes back, Rowena says, 'I suddenly feel very old.'

Celeste laughs.

'No, I do, thinking back to that day. People think I'm younger than I am. Perhaps I've never really grown up, I don't know. I suppose I don't really think about it that much and I just assume I'm the same age as other people and then I realise with a jolt that I'm old enough to be their mother. It's scary. The irony is, because of some of the jobs I've done, I've actually lived the life of an old person before my time, become part of that world. I've got nothing to show for my life.'

'No need to scratch your arms, not everything is tangible. I expect you've made a lot of people's lives easier and happier. Can't you be proud of that?'

She can see Pipe-Cleaner Man lying in his curtained front room. It's a parallel universe, the world of hospital transport that doesn't turn up, meals on wheels, painful infirmities and indignities. Days lit by low-wattage light bulbs and warmed by one-bar electric fires and measured out in pills and dressings and patent remedies, at the mercy of a procession of strangers earning less than the minimum wage. Have Celeste and Francis any idea of how lucky they are?

'Not really,' she says. 'Look at you; the Nautilus, all the other buildings you've done, the social housing Rachel was talking about. Not to mention your family.'

The Natterjack pickup pulls up by the front door. Rowena hopes they will use the cheap mugs and tea bags she has put out for them, and Celeste recalls a disturbing telephone conversation with Lyris, who said, 'Jacki's fine, she's got real flair, but Nathan – well – just don't let him anywhere near the studios. Say they're all let out if he discovers them. I don't want him getting any ideas. My dear great-nephew is entirely without talent as an artist, he made a pig's ear of art school, but I'm sure they'll make a success of the business if Jacki can keep him on the straight and narrow. And, Celeste, I probably shouldn't say this – in fact, I'm sure it isn't necessary now – but do be a little bit careful about leaving your purse lying around.'

Nathan has draped himself in a dust sheet and is dancing around and wailing like a ghost.

'I grew up with many advantages,' Celeste goes on. 'My father was a doctor, my mother a psychologist. I had loving brothers and sisters. We lived in a big house on Haverstock Hill which was always full of fascinating people and I had a wonderful husband. But be that as it may, I suppose we always do think about our age when we've got a birthday coming up.'

'I guess so. What? How did you know?'

'I didn't. Just a shot in the dark. When is it then?'

'Soonish. But I don't celebrate it. I hate my birthday.'

'Isn't that rather a slur on the memory of your parents, and your aunt?'

'Hmm. Well, I'd better get on, I'm supposed to be doing Francis's room. By the way, I do realise that you also had a great talent, which I don't. I wasn't trying to suggest that I could have been an architect if I'd wanted to.'

'I know. You were going to tell me something intriguing about Gus. I'm worried about him, you know. He's losing his *joie de vivre*. I think he's very unhappy – he's so obviously a family man.'

Rowena tells her the story. 'But,' she concludes, 'I vaguely remember a row. Something went missing. One of Gus's toy spanners, I think it might have been. Somebody pinched it. All par for the course.'

There was an episode Rowena recalled more vividly, which occurred in her second year at Chestnuts, before her emotions and perceptions had been dulled by term after succeeding term which never ended in a holiday for her. Other children came and went, teachers took up residence and often disappeared without warning; there was one, Myfanwy, whose departure left a dreadful void, when she packed her bags after a run-in with

Mr Perry who, apart from Mrs Diggins, was the only permanent fixture on the staff. Myfanwy was a gentle girl who taught music, Latin and needlework, and Rowena blossomed for a few weeks in her orderly classes; Mr Perry was an alcoholic who had found that the school's timetable did not impose too much on his own.

On this particular afternoon Rowena had come upon Wendy in the garden with her mending basket.

'"Stitch! stitch! stitch! / In poverty, hunger and dirt,"' she remarked conversationally. '"With fingers weary and worn, / With eyelids heavy and red, / A woman sat in unwomanly rags, / Plying her needle and thread."'

'Rowena! There's no call for that. I am merely replacing a button on Cliff's shirt!'

'"O! men with sisters dear, / O! men with mothers and wives! / It is not linen you're wearing out / But human creatures' lives!" You want to put a proper shank on that, or it will tear,' Rowena told her, quoting Myfanwy and proud of her new skills. 'I'll show you how if you like.'

She took the shirt from Wendy's unresisting hands. '"Sewing at once with a double thread a shroud as well as a shirt. But why do I talk of death? That phantom of grisly bone, I hardly fear his terrible shape, it seem so like my own." I can do buttonholes too.'

'Oh, shut up, you horrible, horrible morbid little show-off! I'm sick to death of you. If your wretched aunt hadn't been so inconsiderate you wouldn't be here at all. Who do you imagine pays to keep you fed and clothed? You might be able to twist Clifford round your little finger but you don't fool me for one moment. You want to do buttonholes? Then do buttonholes. You can do all these damned shirts!'

She picked up the mending basket and emptied it, pins, needles, cotton reels and all, over Rowena's head.

If her aunt had known what Wendy was really like, she would never have been friends with her, Rowena thought at the time. Now she concedes that if you had Wendy Waddilove's life, a child spouting Thomas Hood at you and teaching you to sew on buttons might have been the last straw. She hadn't meant to show off though, and she had never spoken poetry aloud since. Wendy had tried to be nice again later on; perhaps she was afraid Rowena would tell Cliff, or possibly she was ashamed, but they both knew she had said things which could never be unsaid.

She was as crushed by humiliation then as she was when Bernadette demanded back the keys. Soon after the 'Song of the Shirt' incident, she had fallen ill, with a high fever, and in her delirium she believed she was one of the school toys, a rag doll called Lindy-Lou with a broken squeaker in its chest.

Badly done, Francis, badly done. His attempt at gallantry with Belle had been so ill-judged and might well poison her declining years, or even hasten her to the grave. The poor old thing hadn't looked well at all. No doubt he would be crossing Belle's name out of his address book before the year was out. He must make an effort to make amends in such time as she had left. Francis is working on his memoirs in his chamber which seems much lighter since Rowena cleaned the patina of nicotine from the walls. 'Belle De Groot', he has written so far, 'was one of the great beauties of her generation and is a greater poet than many whose work is better known. I'll never forget our first meeting at the Café Royal' – or was it at the Gargoyle? He has no memory whatsoever of their first meeting but he can remember Belle dancing down Old Compton Street with a sailor on either arm. It is hard to capture the essence of Belle; he is striving to evoke her captivating blend of poetic seriousness and gaiety, generosity and courage, but the right words elude him. It's like trying to trap the scents of a summer garden in a bottle. How he detests writing nowadays and his concentration isn't helped by Nathan and Jacki larking about below his window, flicking paint brushes at each other and shrieking. Celeste was crazy to take them on, when any fool could have told her she should have got a proper surveyor in first. He can't remember if he had. Rowena appears to have thrown out that ink he was distilling from oak apples; now he will never know if the experiment would have worked. It would be so much easier just to horsewhip the fellow who had traduced Belle, but he owed it to her, and to posterity, to set the record straight.

There was a summer when he and Belle played at being engaged, with a ring from Woolworths. It was just as well they hadn't married; he doesn't know how Belle would have fitted in at the Nautilus, and the truth is that he has been perfectly happy in his long companionship with Celeste, since Arkady died. Also, it's a sad fact that Belle, though younger, has not aged nearly as well as he has. He wonders if she will merit a memorial service; that will be a sad occasion. Sadder if she doesn't. He had taken it for granted once that he would have one but now he's not so sure. Like the invitation to appear on *Desert Island Discs* that never came. There aren't many left to attend his funeral. He imagines it will be a fairly paltry affair, with just a handful of people and 'Sailing By'. Unless Celeste puts a three-line whip on the family for appearances' sake.

Belle's still got all her marbles though, which makes it imperative that he get on with this blasted memoir. Assuming anybody will publish it. He supposes he'll have to send Belle the appropriate extract, ostensibly to ask her opinion of it. Weird though, her running after them with that bit of spider plant. Was it a spontaneous gesture of friendship to Rowena, had she been giving her blessing to him and Rowena as a couple, was there some sarcastic intent, or had she gone slightly loopy after all? Too much to hope she has, and won't ferret out the meaning of his thoughtless words.

Trouble is, he's expended all his creative energy on a letter to Magnus regretting that he won't be able to travel up to his birthday celebration, and he still hasn't written anything for the Festschrift. Now that he needs a piece of unpublished poetry, his juvenilia has deserted him and he can't recall a single line. Time is running out, but even a haiku or a limerick is beyond him. Such a pity that Rowena turned out not to be a secret scribbler. He has tried sitting at his desk in Louis MacNeice's hat, but even that failed to inspire him. Celeste thought that her crack about the Queen's Poetry Medal had fallen on deaf ears, but it wounded him deeply.

No chance of old Magnus making it to his funeral. If Francis feels he can't cope with the journey to Scotland, how can he expect Magnus to do the same thing in reverse, even if Jeanie were to accompany him, which she wouldn't because she had always been a little jealous of Magnus's friendship with Francis. How long ago it was, how long ago, that he and Magnus had first met in the BBC club just before Magnus went off to fight with the International Brigade in Spain.

He supposes that some folk might find even Norwood Cemetery too far to travel to – people are so snobbish about crossing the river. Perhaps a minibus could be laid on, if the mourners were to assemble at DAMS. A charabanc of the despondent and mad. It would be wiser to have it at Golders Green if he wants a halfway decent turnout. No doubt somebody would read one of his poems. 'Poppets', inevitably.

'Will you stop that infernal racket!' He flings up the window and shouts. 'I am trying to work and you are driving me mad!'

His voice stops Nathan and Jacki in their tracks. They look up at him, open-mouthed. Nathan has been chasing Jacki with a hosepipe and water sprays on to the ground.

'What's your problem, Gramps?' says Nathan.

'Right, that's it. You're fired! Your contract is terminated as from now.'

Francis grabs his walking stick and takes the stairs as fast as he can.

'Go, on, get out of here!' he yells, waving his stick. 'You useless pair of time-wasting toads. Pack up your things and go. I've had quite enough of your intolerable noise.'

'Please – we're really sorry. We'll be quiet, I promise. We didn't realise we were disturbing you.' Jacki looks as if she's about to burst into tears.

Francis would have backed down then, if Nathan had not said, 'You can't tell us what to do, you miserable old git. Everybody knows Mrs Zee's the one that wears the trousers round here.'

Francis rushes at him, lashing out wildly and catching Nathan a glancing blow on the arm.

'You bastard. You hit me. I'll have you for that. Come on, Jack, we're not staying here. He ought to be locked up.'

Later, Celeste comes to his room. 'Have you seen the Natterjacks? They seem to have disappeared. Most unprofessional.'

Francis gives a sly smile. 'They have folded their dust sheets like the Arabs, and as silently stolen away.'

Gus helps his customer to carry her purchase to the car which is illegally parked half on the pavement outside the shop. The mahogany wine cooler is heavy, with its lead liner intact, and lion's mask handles and lion's paw feet. He should be pleased with the sale but the transaction reminds him of the first time Lois came into the shop, looking for a present for her husband's birthday, poor bloke. She'd left it until the last moment and grabbed a decanter with a set of glasses as if she didn't much care what she bought. This wasn't really her part of town; she lived over in Dulwich Village but she'd come up this way for some reason. Slumming, he thinks now. Lois had dropped in several times after that and eventually she'd invited him for a drink at her house. The rest is history.

It had really amused him though, that for all her willowy elegance, she had this cute way of taking off her jumper, pulling it over her head like a little boy. But that doesn't weigh up against what he'd lost as a result. He decides to bite the bullet and ring his mum to get her to intervene with Carole, and if that doesn't work, he'll go round and demand reasonable access to the children. It's his right. They need him, even if he has let them down. He can't bear that they might think he doesn't care about them any more. He's written to them and sent a parcel of sweets and comics, but he's heard nothing back.

Funny, when he was carrying the wine cooler to the car, looking down the road in case the traffic warden was about, he'd thought he'd seen Rhiannon with a couple of boys, and it crossed his mind that they might be coming here. He goes to the door just in time to see Rhiannon disappearing into Urban Blight's premises.

'Oi!'

Too late. Locking his own door, Gus strides into the shop next door, pushing his way past various smelly garments hanging around, and into the back of the shop.

'Gus! What are you doing here?'

Her school blouse is unbuttoned, pulled down to expose her shoulder. Urban's got a needle in his own red-and-blue spiderwebbed hand, all his paraphernalia is spread out on a table and two schoolboys are perched on stools, crammed up against the lurid posters on the walls. There is a heap of bags on the floor.

'Shouldn't you lot be in school?'

'What's it to you?' says Urban. 'You can't just barge in here interfering with my customers.' He's wearing a vest, exposing the artwork on his skinny chest.

'Yes I can. Do you know how old she is? Do you even care? Rhiannon, does your mum know about this? Of course she doesn't, does she? Are you insane? You must know the risks of infected needles.'

'Here, watch what you're saying. I'll have you know I've got a licence,' whines Urban. 'I'm a certified tattoo artist.'

Rhiannon is rolling down her sleeve over her young unblemished arm, looking terrified.

'You won't grass me up to Mum, Gus, will you? She'd go mad. Promise you won't tell her. Please!'

'Get your bag. You're going back to school even if I have to drive you there myself. Is this one yours?'

He picks up a schoolbag.

'Oi, that's my bag! Who do you think you are anyway?'

Gus drops the bag, and as he does, he sees a can of red spray paint. He picks it up and examines it.

'This colour looks familiar.'

The boy grabs his bag and tries to escape but Gus blocks his way. Rhiannon is crying.

The other kid snickers nervously. 'We was only having a laugh.'

Gus pictures the scene, the wrecked car, the scattered picnic things, the condom.

'Honestly, Gus, it wasn't me, I swear. There was a whole gang of us. I tried to stop them. Didn't I, Damian? Tell him I tried to stop you! I wouldn't let you touch the van, would I? Don't go to the police, Gus, it would kill my mum. I'm begging you. Please don't grass us up. I'll do anything you like. Anything.'

'What's going on?' says Urban Blight.

'Right, you lot. School, now! While I decide what I'm going to do. And you,' he turns to Urban, 'if I find you've been supplying drugs to schoolkids, you're for the chop, mate. Rhiannon, I'll expect you, and your mates, at the Nautilus at six o'clock sharp, and don't even think about not showing up.'

The telephone is ringing in the hall. It is not used much because all the residents have their own phone. Rowena answers it, knowing it won't be for her.

'Hello? Who is that please? Rowena? Oh good. Gus isn't there, is he?'

It is Izzie. Rowena had managed to block her out, and here she is, rearing her ugly head again. What fresh hell is this?

'No, he isn't.'

'Never mind. I just wanted to thank him for all his kindness.'

'How are the knees?'

'Oh, fine thank you. I'd forgotten about them. I wanted to thank you too, of course. I won't be using the scooter again though. I've bought a car. The thing is, I've got to go and collect my daughter Miranda from the airport. She's got glandular fever. I'm bringing her home. Which means I've had to put all my plans on hold indefinitely.'

* * *

'That was Izzie on the phone,' Rowena tells Celeste. 'Her daughter's got glandular fever. She sounded really happy about it.'

She does a little dance with her Vileda mop.

'I can't understand the Natterjacks' behaviour,' says Celeste. 'I wouldn't have thought it of Jacki at least. So much for the Color Kittens. But it's rather a relief, to tell you the truth. I was beginning to wonder if they were up to the job. And isn't it blissfully peaceful without their wretched radio?' Then she adds wistfully, 'Of course, the Nautilus was filled with music in the old days. My husband once said that if you put it to your ear like a seashell, you would hear music instead of the sound of the waves.'

Time has exposed a flaw in their design, for whereas the marine inhabitant of the pearly nautilus seals off each chamber when it becomes too large for it, and constructs another, she had grown too small for her shell.

Rowena catches a glimpse of Heligoland, a shimmer of grey on the horizon.

'Are you around on Sunday? Rachel and family are coming, and perhaps some of the others and it would be nice if you were here.'

'I'm going to see somebody after lunch, but I expect I'll be back by about four. Do you want me to make something for tea?'

'Don't worry. Rachel will probably bring something, or we can have *sauve qui peut*.'

Rowena laughs. She is too nervous about her own plan for Sunday to angst about meeting 'some of the others'. She thinks about Izzie. Obviously she has realised where her duty lies, but she wouldn't put it past her to turn up again like a mendicant friar sometime in the future.

Later that evening, Celeste is walking in the grounds. A bramble catches her skirt and she stoops to disentangle it. When she looks up, she sees a peculiar sight. Gus and three teenagers are walking towards her, one of them pushing the old wheelbarrow full of gardening tools. Can they be Gus's children? They look too grown up. The girl is very pretty.

'What's all this?' she asks when they reach her.

'Call it a youth employment scheme if you like. Or community service,' says Gus.

12

It is Sunday morning. Rowena goes into the garden to pick some chives for the potato salad she has made to leave for the others; she herself is much too anxious about the afternoon to want any lunch. She can see Francis a short distance away, sitting on a chair in the grass, wearing his brown dressing gown. A squirrel making little runs towards him, stopping to check that it's safe and then running closer, reaches Francis and sits up, crossing its paws on its white chest. It's between his bare feet, shod in the shoes of the fisherman. He doesn't move. Rowena holds her breath as a bird flies down and flutters for a second on to Francis's head. She smiles; he looks just like a statue of St Francis of Assisi, sitting so still in his brown dressing gown. But he is too still.

She runs towards him. The squirrel looks at her with dark liquid eyes, flicks its tail and spirals up the trunk of a tree. Francis's eyes are closed. Tentatively, Rowena touches his hand, fearing it will be stiff and cold.

'Ah, Rowena, I've been dreaming.'

His hand feels papery and warmed by the sun. His dressing gown is flecked with croissant crumbs and his spectacles are lying in his lap.

Oh, Francis. I thought you were dead. 'What were you dreaming about?'

'Dandy? Oh – I thought Dandy had come back to

me. I was so happy . . .' His eyes fill with tears. 'And Magnus was there. I do wish I could see him again but I must just accept that I never will. I've left it too late and now I'm not up to the journey.'

As he is speaking, Rowena pictures two little dogs, Dandy and Frenchie, wearing frills round their necks like circus dogs, and jumping through paper hoops. It is so sad for Francis that all his happiness lies in the past. When he was telling her about his dream though, she wondered if he had actually experienced a foretaste of heaven. But she cannot bear the thought of him not being here any more. She kneels down beside his chair.

'I'm so sorry I spoiled your dream. But you could see Magnus again. You could if I came with you. I'll come, Francis, if you want me to. I don't mind making the travel arrangements. We could fly there.'

Francis clutches her hand. 'You wouldn't, would you? I can't believe it, Rowena. You'd really come with me?'

She nods.

'Perhaps we could fly, but I think we might have to take a ferry on the final stage of the journey.'

The lines from Yeats come back to him in joyful affirmation. 'To an isle in the water with her I would fly.'

What have I done? Rowena thinks. I've never been inside a travel agent's in my life. I don't know *how* to go to a travel agent. They are for other people, real people who go on holiday, and don't have to lie to hairdressers. I've never been to an airport. I won't know what to do. And Magnus Scrabster, and all those people. And what clothes should I take? Supposing there's a ceilidh?

I can't do Scottish dancing. I'll have to sprain my ankle getting off the ferry.

'There's something I've been meaning to tell you,' says Francis. 'You expressed an interest in Heligoland, didn't you? Well, the other night, sometime in the early hours when I couldn't sleep, I heard a strange piece of music on the wireless, for male voices and orchestra. Turned out to be called *Helgoland*. By Bruckner. Just thought you'd like to know.'

Carrying the delphiniums she'd bought at the flower stall from a man who looked disconcertingly like an older version of Nathan Natterjack, and fortified by a couple of Quiet Life tablets, Rowena walks through the Belfairs Estate in the Sunday afternoon heat-haze, just as she used to do twice daily, past a car with no wheels slumped on the asbestos, past the adventure playground where the only occupant is a small girl swinging in a tyre on a rope, hearing the call of a tropical bird and, through an open window, the clashing of plates as somebody washes up their lunch things. The sound takes her back to Formosa Road where she had lived to the rhythm of other people's lives, inhaled the smells of her neighbours' Sunday dinners and barbecues, listened to their music, and their voices in the gardens, the noises of their lawnmowers and hedge strimmers. Their lives seemed much more real than hers, so much more valid somehow, that she sometimes felt she had no right to be there at all, and when the house was quiet late at night, she dared not use her electric toothbrush for fear of annoying them and she played her radio under the duvet like a schoolgirl. And of course it was she who cleared the junk mail, dropped tissues and dead leaves from the hall.

She rings the bell of Mr Apsley's flat, dreading that Derek will come to the door. She rings again. Something in the bell's tone tells her that there is nobody at home. But that's impossible, Mr Apsley never goes out. Unless –

'They've taken him into King's.'

It is his next-door neighbour, Mrs Malarkey, in a pink dressing gown.

'Do you know which ward?'

'Trundle and Waddington, I think. I'd like to go and visit him myself only . . .'

Only you'd have to get dressed. 'Thanks, Mrs Malarkey. Nice to see you.'

The little girl is still swinging in a desultory way on the car tyre as Rowena retraces her steps.

Sitting on the bus to King's College Hospital, she notices a travel agent's with bright posters in the window. That is the next ordeal she will have to face, but she will think about it when she's got through this one. The dread day of her birthday falls next week and Celeste's suggestion that by hating her birthday, she is dishonouring her parents and Aunt Mysie has been troubling her too.

Rowena is familiar with the hospital, having visited several other clients there in the past. She walks past the massive rebuilding project, still in progress, past the cluster of smokers hooked up to drips and in wheelchairs outside the entrance, and into the reception area. There's the cash machine where she's sometimes drawn out money for patients, the pharmacy where she's sat for hours waiting for people's prescriptions, the smell of the café round the corner from the flower shop, the drinks machine. King's is a city unto itself and its citizens throng the thoroughfares. She stops off at Forbuoys' to buy a box of peppermint creams and, heart pounding, takes the stairs to the ward, resisting the temptation to seek sanctuary in the chapel instead. She could sit there with a cup of coffee, looking at the beautiful stained glass, and perhaps shedding a tear at the memorial book where bereaved people write messages to their loved ones.

There is no need to ask a nurse where Mr Apsley is because the first person she sees on entering is Derek. He is sitting on the chair beside the bed, watching another patient's television. He starts when he sees Rowena and she sees that he is scared of her. So he should be after what he's done to her. But what's he doing here, when his father knows he was stealing from him?

Mr Apsley's bed is next to the nurses' station, which is usually a bad sign, but he looks rosier than the last time she saw him.

His face lights up. 'Rowena!'

'Hullo,' she says, taking the hand he is holding out to her. 'I see you've got some new pyjamas.'

'Derek got these in Morley's sale, didn't you, son? Are those flowers for me? Don't just sit there, Derek, get the lady a vase. Go on then, you'll find them in the sluice room.'

Derek is wearing a short-sleeved yellow nylon shirt which accentuates his breasts and gives off a faint smell of lard. As soon as he has gone, looking daggers at her,

Mr Apsley says hurriedly, 'I'm sorry about that other business. I never thought it was you, but, well – Derek's a good boy really. He always intended to pay it back.'

He beams at his son when he returns with a glass jar which had once contained tomato juice.

'Well done, son,' he says, as if Derek has done something really clever in finding that jar, which Rowena has to concede, from her own hospital visiting experiences, he has.

'Will you come and see me again, when they let me out of here?'

'Of course I will. It won't be for a while though because I'm going up to Scotland with a friend,' she tells him, arranging the flowers and putting them on top of his locker. She notices his slippers, splashed with dried soup, in a sticky pool of orange juice and dust under the bed.

'Bonnie Scotland, eh? Hoots, mon, och aye the noo –' A fit of coughing seizes him, its violence jolting him from the pillow. 'He wouldn't be male by any chance, this friend of yours?' he wheezes when he can speak again, lying back exhausted and grey but managing a wink.

'He might. See you soon. Take care.' She bends to gives him a peck on the top of his head.

'Goodbye, Derek.'

She holds out her hand and Derek takes it, squeezing hard, looking into her eyes, conveying the message that she will not be seeing his father again.

'Hang on a minute, Rowena. I'd like to give you a little something for your trip.'

Mr Apsley gropes around in the shelf of his bedside locker and his fingers close on something.

'Here we are. This will do.'

He hands her the box of peppermint creams she brought him.

'You enjoy these with your friend.' He winks.

As she approaches the Nautilus, Rowena sees two people, a man and a woman, having an argument in the street. She crosses over, but as she gets closer she sees that the woman is Rita. What on earth is she doing here? She must be coming to see Gus, but as far as Rowena knows, it's for the first time. The man is quite small, with a little beard, and wearing a jeans jacket and faded jeans.

'You evil hobbit, how dare you be my daughter's father!' Rita is yelling.

The man grabs her arm, laughing. 'Come on, Reet, give us a chance. Let bygones be bygones, eh?'

Rowena pretends she hasn't seen them, and hurries on. A taxi passes her and she glimpses a white-haired old lady in the back seat. It could almost be Belle De Groot, who had thrust the spider plant on her. When she turns in to the drive, there are several cars parked there, and she can hear voices coming from the garden and the shouts of children. She had completely forgotten that Celeste's family were coming to tea. She can't face them yet and sneaks round the side of the building, through the laundry door. She goes upstairs, wanting to sit quietly and reflect on making her peace with Mr Apsley. All the way home, she had felt peculiar, light-headed with gratitude that she had been given the chance to say goodbye, and had longed to be alone with her thoughts in the garden.

Her door is ajar. She is certain that she left it shut. As

soon she as enters the room she senses a loss. All is tidy as she left it but something is missing. Angus. He's gone. He is not on the bed or the window sill. She stands in the middle of the room, paralysed by panic. Her arms start itching and she sways back and forth on her feet as scenes from Angus's life pass through her mind in rapid succession.

Then she knows. Gus has stolen him. He has taken Angus to sell in his shop. She remembers him examining the label on Angus's foot, as if he knew he was worth something. Gus lied to her; he doesn't just find things, he takes them too. How could he betray her, after finding their shared past? Rowena rushes down the stairs and outside, to find Celeste, to tell her what's happened and ask if she knows where Gus is.

She stops in her tracks, gripping the anchor. The garden has turned into a crowded beach, with old people wearing sunhats in deckchairs on the shingle, younger people sitting on picnic rugs in the marram grass, and sprawling on the softer grass beyond, babies who have brought their own chairs, children shrieking in the spray from the hosepipe, a toddler in swimming trunks pouring pebbles from a plastic bucket, a frisbee skimming the air.

'Here she is. Hurrah!' calls Celeste, clapping her hands, and throwing her straw hat in the air.

Somebody else joins in, and then they're all clapping as she walks towards them. It's terrible. Her face is on fire.

'Happy Unbirthday!' says Celeste. 'We thought you deserved a little celebration as a small thank you for all that you've done for the Nautilus, for bringing it to life again, and your unfailing generosity to us all.'

'Hear, hear!' Francis says. Belle De Groot, it is she sitting next to him, echoes him vaguely, and so does Rachel, heartily.

Paul is there, smearing sunblock on Evie, and Rita and the hobbit, but who are all these other people, the men in linen jackets, women in silk print frocks and sundresses, half-naked children in shorts, all looking expectantly at her? One elderly man, is it Konstantin, is holding a violin. This is hideous, a nightmare, they don't know her at all. Can't they see that she's really a horrible person? What did Celeste say about bringing the Nautilus to life again? Where's Angus, locked in a junk shop, or even sold already, beyond rescue? She has spotted Gus, in a Hawaiian shirt and sunglasses, and strides up to accuse him.

'Don't just stand there like two of eels, come and sit down,' he says. 'Meet the family.' A boy and girl are jostling for space on his knees and he's resting his hand on a woman's blonde head.

'What have you done with Angus?' She speaks at last.

'Who? Oh, the doll. Hope you don't mind, Kizzy wandered into your room by mistake. Casing the joint. Celeste's invited Carole and the kids to move in, till we get ourselves sorted. Sailor Boy's over there.'

She looks. In the shade of a tree is a long table spread with a white cloth and crowded with party food. At its centre stands an enormous iced cake decorated with what looks like gummed paper shapes and a single candle. Beside it, propped up against a jug of Pimm's, is Angus.

'Looks like he's having a good time. Bit of a lad, isn't he?'

'No, he isn't. Angus has never been like that,' she retorts.

Then she gives an uncertain laugh, at her own words. Angus's sailor hat is on at a jaunty angle and he does look as if he's having a good time. A bit tipsy in fact. Perhaps he ought to get out more.

Violet runs up to her. 'We made the cake in honour of you.'

She is wearing a party dress and two sparkly slides in her hair.

Then Rowena sees the solution to one dilemma, 'Actually, Celeste, you have got the right day. Today *is* my birthday. You're a genius. I'm overwhelmed,' she says in a monotone.

But Celeste is gazing straight past her.

'Jenners! Come and join us. So glad you could make it. You're just in time for the cutting of the cake.'

Jenners Leaf is walking across the grass, holding a bunch of flowers.

It is all too much. Rowena sits down on the grass. She doesn't know how to have a birthday party. She can't deal with flowers and a birthday cake. How could this have gone on behind her back without her knowing anything about it? She's supposed to be the housekeeper here. Somebody has dragged out the stack of ancient deckchairs and cleaned off the cobwebs, but they aren't safe; the canvas will give way and people will be trapped. Gus hands her a glass of Pimm's.

'Rita, would your daughter and her friends like to join us now?' says Celeste, explaining to the company at large, while the little man in the jeans jacket scrambles eagerly to his feet, 'Rita's lovely daughter Rhiannon and her friends are clearing out the swimming pool, won't that be fun, and then they want to make a start on the vegetable garden. It's wonderful to find young people willing to give up their time so unselfishly, and with a real interest in gardening. One only ever hears the bad things about the younger generation. Oh, Lyris, I didn't mean . . .'

The legendary Lyris Crane gives a caustic laugh, then starts, spilling her drink, as a voice behind her says, 'Gang's all here, I see. Hullo, Aunty. Mrs Zee. Can me and Jacki come to your party? We'll be ever so good.'

Nathan catches the flying frisbee and, grinning, holds it aloft, a yellow disc like the sun against the blue sky. Behind him, Jacki, covered in embarrassment, is apologising profusely.

'Honestly, we'd no idea you were having company. We never meant to intrude. We just wanted to sort things out, but we'll go. Come on, Nathan, we're leaving! Now!'

'Sit down and have a drink, dear,' says Celeste. 'The more the merrier.'

Francis emits a low growl, like a dog baring its teeth.

'So you and Francis are off to Scotland?' Lyris, resolutely ignoring her great-nephew, says to Rowena.

Rowena can see herself and Francis leaning on the rail of the ferry, sailing through calm silver seas, a few gulls circling, the Hebrides or Heligoland far away in a misty shimmer on the horizon. How peaceful it is; no sound but the gentle slap of waves on the sides of the boat and the cries of the birds. But as she looks round at them all, in the noisy garden of the Nautilus, it comes to her that perhaps here are her people, come for her at last.

Nevertheless, as she travelled home on the bus, she couldn't get out of her mind that little girl swinging in the tyre, all alone. Somebody should have been looking after her. Somebody ought to have been standing behind her to give the swing a push, and to catch her in their arms when she jumped off. It occurred to Rowena then that if she could face going into a travel agent's, she might as well pick up some brochures about travelling to India someday in the future. It would be the first tentative step on the long journey to find her family. For all she knows there might be a child somewhere who needs her, who is waiting for her to come. She can't think of a better way to honour Aunt Mysie.

For the first time, the tantalising flashes of colour on the edges of her memory that have always eluded her seem within her grasp. And what was the point of fretting over her aunt's lost possessions when in some churchyard there must be an unvisited grave, weeds to clear, a headstone to be set, a white rose to be planted?

Meanwhile, there is this party to get through, and it is the least she can do to look as though she is enjoying it. People are moving towards the table. Violet's hairslides glitter in the sun, Jenners is putting the flame of his cigarette lighter to the candle on the cake. Sparkle, Shirley, sparkle! Rowena doesn't know how to have birthday parties, but suddenly it all seems to be going quite well.